I0687445

Killer Cruise

by

Marilyn Baron

A Psychic Crystal Mystery
Book Three

Killer Cruise

Cover Art by *Debbie Taylor*

The Wild Rose Press, Inc.
PO Box 708
Adams Basin, NY 14410-0708
Visit us at www.thewildrosepress.com

Publishing History
First Crimson Rose Edition, 2015
Print ISBN 978-1-62830-834-1
Digital ISBN 978-1-62830-835-8

A Psychic Crystal Mystery, Book Three

She tried to fight her feelings, but, she had to admit, the Chief was making her feel something. Something monumental.

Some couples walking by clapped. The men gave Will a thumbs-up.

Finally, he let her go.

"Don't do that again," Juliette hissed, straightening the sleeve of her dress from where it had slipped off her shoulder.

"It felt good, didn't it, sugar?" Will challenged.

"Maybe to you, but not to me." Juliette colored, and she made a show of smoothing the wrinkles out of her wrinkle-free dress. She wondered if the Chief knew she was lying.

"Just let go, Juliette. You're so uptight. You know you felt something. Let's see where it takes us."

"I know where it's going to take us. Nowhere. And if you kiss me like that again, you'll be sorry."

"Now don't go getting your feathers all ruffled. What are you going to do, turn me into a frog?"

Juliette mustered up her most malevolent glare and fixed him with her cold-as-steel violet eyes. "Don't tempt me, Will Bradley. You don't want to mess with me. I killed a man, remember?"

"A man who deserved to die," Will said. "Someday, I'd like to hear the story, from you."

"Instead of the tabloids? Well, I killed him, and I'd do it again. Just mull that over, next time you decide to paw me in public," Juliette threatened.

Praise for Marilyn Baron

"Baron offers a bit of everything.... There's humor, infidelity, murder, mayhem, and a neatly drawn conclusion."

~RT Book Reviews (4.5 Stars)

"An enjoyable read from start to finish...family, friends, enemies, intrigue and suspense...sadness, laughter, romance and ultimately love."

~Romance Junkies (4 Blue Ribbons)

"*SIXTH SENSE* has a great mix of romance, spine-tingling suspense, and real hope for two jaded individuals for a happily-ever-after ending. I'm looking forward to reading Book Two in the Psychic Crystal Mystery Series."

~Tami Brothers

"An intriguing, albeit reluctant, psychic detective in this paranormal romantic suspense story...a strong and captivating heroine."

~Pauline Michael, Night Owl Romance (3 Stars)

"I just finished reading *UNDER THE MOON GATE* and really enjoyed it. I was fascinated by the intertwining of the characters in the stories from the 1700s to present day and I especially enjoyed the segment that took place during WWII. Great writing. Marilyn did a great job of bringing Bermuda during the WWII era to life in this book."

~PJ Ausdenmore, The Romance Dish

"[*UNDER THE MOON GATE*] is a surefire blockbuster...a treasure trove of mystery and intrigue. It sparkles with romance.... I couldn't recommend it more."

~Andrew Kirby

Dedication

To my wonderful family
who support me in everything I do—
Steve, Marissa and Amanda

Chapter One

Juliette Spencer's bedroom violet eyes drilled holes in the ill-mannered boor leering at her breasts like he was stalking his prey or scoping out his next meal. Like he wanted to inhale her or impale her or worse. Like she was Bambi and it was open season on single women sporting a deer-in-the-headlights demeanor.

How did the rutting buck's horns manage to stay atop his swelled head? His buff body filled to capacity the stateroom they would be sharing for the next two weeks, and his looming presence violated her personal space. The overpowering odor of the brute's aftershave was stifling in such close quarters. This suite wasn't big enough for both of them. And there was no escape, short of jumping off the ship, which she had half a mind to do. She could go out on the balcony and breathe in the night air, but she was trapped—"married" to this bozo for the remainder of the cruise.

Juliette knew exactly what the Chief was thinking. And it made her blush. Being psychic had its advantages *and* disadvantages. He was thinking he could have her anytime he wanted. All he had to do was flash that hundred-watt smile of his and flex those overdeveloped muscles, barely disguised in his body-hugging Graysville Police Department T-shirt. She turned away and found herself gazing at his image in the cheval mirror, which only made matters worse.

(*Objects in the mirror are closer than they appear.*)

Well, he could think again. She wasn't going to go all gooey over a green-eyed small-town lawman. This was business, and the Chief apparently had plans to combine this assignment with pleasure, *his* pleasure.

No doubt he knew all about her tainted history of living among a secret society of psychics in the quaint spiritualist community of Casa Spirito, Florida, and her sordid relationship with the trance medium and cult leader Reverend Carter Coulter. The whole world knew about it. It had happened practically in this man's own backyard. So of course he thought he knew her and what she'd be willing to do for him and to him. And the fact that she could read him like a book didn't leave much to anyone's imagination.

Blowing out a breath, she turned on him. She'd just have to make do, dismiss the dimples, and ignore the abs. This was an opportunity to get to know her daughter better and, after they solved the mystery, spend a relaxing cruise with Kate and Kate's new husband, Jack. Distasteful as he was, the Chief or Sheriff or whatever his rank, was part of the package. Andy of Mayberry he was not. Not a redeeming bone in his sculpted body.

Will had seemed polite enough when she first met him at a barbecue in Atlanta at The Crystal Palace, the mansion Kate had inherited on her parents' death, and where Juliette, Jack, and Kate now lived and worked at the Crystal & Hale agency. Will had shown some interest in her, but he must have been on his best behavior. He had worked with Jack and Kate on the Homecoming Homicides case in Graysville, Florida, and for some reason they were anxious for her to meet him. But if they had matchmaking in mind, even if she was looking to fall in love again—which she very definitely was not—Chief Will Bradley was the last man on earth she would lose her heart to.

Chapter Two

The ship's captain was beginning his behind-the-scenes tour of the luxury liner so the investigative team could become familiar with their surroundings.

Will stood behind Juliette, arms wrapped viselike around her waist, close enough so she could feel his hot breath on her neck and his well-defined bulge against her bottom. Whether he was horny for her or that was his perpetual state of arousal, she didn't know him well enough to tell, although, for all the world, they were on their honeymoon. Honeymoon or not, the Chief wasn't going to get his girl, not on this cruise or in any lifetime. Juliette shifted uncomfortably. His grip around her tightened, and she felt him stiffen against her.

"Juliette, sugar, this won't take long." He licked her ear and whispered into it, loud enough for the captain to hear. "Then we can go back to what we were doin' in the cabin."

Juliette shot a venomous gaze over her shoulder.

"Now, baby cakes, are you puttin' a hex on your lovin' husband?"

Juliette scowled and lowered her voice to a barely audible whisper. "Just trying to protect the ship by warding off evil spirits, influences, and malevolent forces."

"We've received a general threat," the captain announced. "We have no idea where it will come from, but we're convinced there's a potential murderer on board this ship. It's our job to find him or her before the ship docks in the next port, if possible. The crew is restless, but they've agreed to stay on the ship for the duration since Crystal Ball Kate is sailing with us. We also offered them hazard pay."

"How do you know there aren't any crew members involved in this plot?" Jack asked.

"That's the problem. We don't. But this crew has been with us the entire season. The officers have been with us for years. We can't rule anyone out, of course, but nobody, including me, gets a free pass in this investigation."

"Jack tells me we have some VIPs on board," said Chief Bradley, who had released Juliette from his tentacles but maintained his connection by holding her hand.

"Yes, we have representatives from the European Union sailing with us in hopes of finalizing an important banking treaty. We're not sure if they are the target of a political threat, but we need to do our best to keep them—and everyone aboard the vessel—safe, by any means, traditional or nontraditional."

"That's why we're here," Jack stated.

"Of course the EU members travel with their own bodyguards, but the more eyes we have on the potential targets, the better. The crew has been reassured by your wife's presence. They're convinced the threat might be of an extrasensory nature. And the fact that we're sailing into the Bermuda Triangle is troubling."

Juliette nodded at Kate. Since she'd been reunited with her daughter, the two had been working closely on growing and controlling Kate's considerable powers, and the girl was coming into her own. They had discussed the Bermuda Triangle, which, according to Juliette, was not of insignificant consequence.

"If there's anything mystical going on, we'll get to the bottom of it," Juliette assured.

Chief Bradley gave *her* bottom a possessive squeeze. "If anyone can get to the bottom of a problem, my wife can."

Juliette jumped and pried the Chief's hand away from its grip on her backside.

"If you don't stop pawing me, I'm going to turn you into a seagull," Juliette whispered venomously.

Chief Bradley sprang back, releasing his hold on Juliette. "Now, honey, no need to resort to black magic."

"You have no idea what I would resort to, and you don't want to find out."

The captain cleared his throat and continued his remarks. "Welcome aboard the *Sea Nymph*. And speaking of hexes, it's not uncommon for fishing boats in the Mediterranean to have stylized evil eyes painted on their bows. Sailors, after all, are a superstitious lot. That's why we don't start a cruise on Fridays. Friday is considered unlucky because that is the day Christ was crucified. The same is true about the first Monday in April."

Will rested his head on Juliette's shoulder. "Why is that?"

"That's the day Cain slew Abel."

"I'm not superstitious," joked Will, reaching around Juliette to knock on the polished wooden railing. "Black cats and ladders, you know."

"In some cultures, black cats are considered good

luck," the captain pointed out. "British and Irish sailors often adopt a black 'ship's cat' because they eat rodents. A ship's cat creates a sense of security for sailors who are away from home for long periods of time."

"Are there rats on this ship?" Kate asked, rubbing her shoulders and looking down.

"Hopefully not." The captain laughed. "But our sailors are from around the world, so each has his own customs. For example, mermaids are usually considered lucky except to British sailors, who think they provoke disaster."

"Mermaids?" Will asked, his interest piqued. "Have you ever seen one?"

"No, although we run into some pretty hot-looking sirens in port."

"You don't really believe in mermaids, do you?"

"Not as a rule," said the captain.

Juliette fingered the amethyst amulet she wore around her neck. "Where I come from, people used to sell white heather to bring good luck."

"That's a Roma tradition, isn't it?" inquired the captain. "Where are you from, Juliette?"

Juliette hesitated. "Hungary," she whispered and then went silent. The location of her homeland was a personal fact she rarely revealed.

Will spun her around in his arms. "I didn't know that. Are you a gypsy? You kind of look like a gypsy. There's a lot about you I don't know. But I want to find out."

"We'll settle this back in our room," Juliette whispered, narrowing her eyes to a deadly sliver.

"Looking forward to it," said the Chief, flashing

his dangerous dimples.

Chief Bradley was taking all the liberties he could get away with while they were in public because she'd shut him down in the bedroom. He was hoping to sweet talk her out of her clothes, and that was not happening. It had been a long time since she'd felt a man's warmth against her body, but she wasn't going to get sucked back into that dangerous emotional vortex. All the Chief's coaxing and talk about how they needed to make it real, not just play the part, was getting him nowhere. She could spot a phony an Irish mile away. The psychic trade was rife with them.

"There's another superstition," said the captain. "Avoid redheads when going to the ship to begin a journey, because people with red hair bring bad luck unless you speak to the redhead before she speaks to you. The same is true for flat-footed people. But then they also say women on board a ship make the sea angry."

"I hope you're not referring to us," Juliette said, looking at Kate.

"I invited you aboard, so no, of course not."

Will couldn't keep his hands or his thoughts to himself. "Isn't it also true that a naked woman on board a ship will calm the sea?"

Juliette pursed her lips and rolled her eyes.

"Actually, your husband's correct," the captain said. "That's why we have naked figureheads at the prow of a ship. And throwing a stone over a ship that is putting out to sea ensures she will never return. Don't look back once your ship has left port or that will bring bad luck. And never step onto a boat with your left foot first or disaster will follow."

"I think we're going a little *overboard* with these superstitions," cautioned Juliette. "Flowers are unlucky onboard a ship. Pouring wine on the deck will bring good luck on a long voyage. The list is endless."

She glanced at her sparkly silver sandals. Kate had been so generous, offering to foot the bill for a brand new, fabulous wardrobe. Juliette didn't have the appropriate clothes in her closet for a cruise. Kate made her promise not to worry about the cost. Jack had assured her that Kate would be reimbursed, that the client—the cruise line—would pay for everything she needed to play her part.

When she had arrived in her suite that afternoon, all the clothes were already hung or placed neatly in her closet. There were dresses and casual outfits, scarves and designer handbags, high heels, low heels, shoes to match every outfit, all in her size. She'd never owned clothes so fine. She wanted to make her new-found daughter proud, and she wasn't going to waste this amazing opportunity to get to know Kate better. This was only the first day of what promised to be a wonderful two weeks.

Chapter Three

"The more familiar you are with the ship and the crew, the better prepared you'll be to react to the unexpected," said the captain. "We're going to begin our tour in the Activity and Entertainment Department. Our cruise experience revolves around a variety of entertainment options, from comedians and dancers to magicians, musicians, jugglers, and vocalists. We even have psychics." The captain directed a look to Juliette. "Our entertainers all perform their specific daily services, but they share the duties of the cruise staff. Which means they also participate in passenger activities like deck games and contests."

"What does it take to become a psychic aboard a ship?" Juliette asked with no little interest.

"Well, the psychics we hire have a phenomenal sense of perception and a verifiable track record. For instance, we ask them to provide a client list and excellent references."

"How can you prove their accomplishments?" Juliette asked.

"We give them an audition," said the captain. "We ask them to do readings on staff members. And they need to be outgoing, because they are putting on a show for the passengers."

"Hmm." Juliette tapped the toe of her sandal on the wooden deck and considered the possibility of working on a cruise ship as a psychic. She could put on a show. She was certainly playing a role now, one of a *happily* married woman on her honeymoon with the biggest horn dog on the planet.

"Are you interested in a psychic position aboard a ship?" the captain asked.

"No, I'm happy where I am. But it sounds like a glamorous job."

"It can be," agreed the captain. "Now I want you to meet Caroline Garrison. Caroline is our stage manager. She calls all the shows. We have a number of production shows staged in a single space. She's in charge of the production cast, including the people who teach salsa and run bingo."

An elfin dark-haired beauty, as lovely as an actress herself, saluted the captain, a sparkle in her eye. She was flitting around the area like a hummingbird, a bundle of energy, directing, coaching, and running lines.

"Our shows have Broadway standing," the captain said proudly. "Right now Caroline is rehearsing a Country Western number. With freestyle cruising, we've expanded our entertainment options to include dinner cabaret shows and some acts with a local flair from our ports of call. We also bring in on-land branded entertainment, acrobatic-type extravaganzas, and well-known entertainers. We're at sea most of the days of a repositioning cruise like this Barcelona-to-Miami route, so we need to increase our entertainment offerings. And we have ten days to transition our creative team, install, and practice the new show. That's one of the reasons people take a transatlantic cruise. There's entertainment day and night. Gambling, spectacular stage shows, comedy shows, dance clubs, bars and lounges, piano bars, live music—we offer it all. As a matter of fact, we were recently voted the Best Ship for Sea Days.

"With more onboard days, passengers can experience a different restaurant every day. And we always offer extra perks, like a complimentary bottle of wine at dinner at our specialty restaurants on the first night of the cruise, onboard savings at our spa, and discounts at the shops. It's all about relaxation. Guests enjoy our fitness center, sports court, pools, and hot tubs instead of a grueling round of excursions. And best of all, you can save almost seventy-five percent on the cost with a repositioning cruise."

"It sounds perfect," Juliette said.

"And since we're relocating the ship to a new region, travelers enjoy exotic ports of call."

Kate raised her hand to get the captain's attention. "Where and when can you go on a repositioning cruise?"

"Well, typically, they're available most months of the year and include such itineraries as Alaska to Hawaii, Alaska to the Mexican Riviera, and trans-Atlantic sailings like this one from the Mediterranean to Miami and the Caribbean or the reverse."

The captain stopped for a moment, then prompted, "So, Caroline, tell our guests more about the ship."

"Structurally, this is like a big steel floating prison in a box."

"A prison?" wondered Juliette. "You mean you're trapped?"

"You'll only feel that way if you're claustrophobic. But we're floating on the open sea, so you have the expanse of the sky and the calming rhythm of the ocean," the captain interjected.

"The crew gets an extra stipend for work in the theater," Caroline explained. "That supplements their income, so they're lining up to volunteer."

The captain went into detail about the special paint treatment and stage requirements—hidden sets, ascending and descending lifts used for scene changes to and from the pit—used by the stars in a show that would run later that evening.

"We use ship terminology in the theaters," explained the captain, pointing toward the stage and the rigging technicians.

"Lights and video 5, 6, 7, and G-O," shouted Caroline.

"How long have these people been with you?" asked Will.

"At least two years, but we have all the records, so you can check that."

"Is the fourteen-day length of this repositioning cruise typical?" Jack wondered.

"The repositioning cruise is normally a longer cruise, from eleven to sixteen days, with a minimum of eight sea days," said the captain. "It's a transatlantic cruise with an average of 2,400 to 2,600 people. Repositioning cruises normally mean you start in one place and finish in another.

"We usually run half full during repositioning. The Miami cruise stops at the Azores, Bermuda, and St. Thomas, with Miami as the final destination. On a normal cruise we're in port almost every day. Like I said, on the repositioning cruise most days are at sea."

"What does the crew do when they're off?"

"They're off Sunday nights. They'll scuba dive,

watch movies, play games."

The captain signaled the group to accompany him. "Now we're leaving the entertainment area, and we'll take the elevator to the main galley."

The party followed the captain into the elevator and got off on Deck 5, Midship.

"The galley is the culinary heart of the vessel," the captain announced. "Our executive chef is in charge of the entire food operation in all the outlets throughout the ship. The food and beverage team is comprised of approximately 880 crew members."

Will whistled.

"We have the main hot galley located on Deck 5. Here, we prepare all the menus for the main dining room and our second dining room. All entrees are cooked and plated just before the wait staff is ready to serve you. We follow basic recipes. We have a roasting station and a soup station, serving to main dining rooms. Then we make sandwiches."

"Where does the crew dine?"

"That's a good question, Jack. All crew dine in various dining rooms—messes—located on Deck 4. There is also a crew internet café, crew recreational area, and gym. Now we're headed for the crew galley, which we call I-95 because it resembles a busy highway.

"The crew galley is located on Deck 4," continued the captain. "There we cook all of the meals for the approximately 1,740 men and women in the crew from more than seventy countries—all under my command. Each of our specialty restaurants has its own galley.

"The crew is divided into three departments. The Deck, led by the staff captain, includes all bridge officers, deck, medical, security, safety, finance, IT, and surveillance departments.

"The Engine department, led by the chief engineer, maintains all mechanical and electrical aspects of the ship," stated the captain. "The Hotel is led by the hotel director and includes all stewards, the cruise director and staff, galley and bar staff."

The captain led the group to the pantry.

"The pantry is the station of the galley where we prepare all the cold appetizers, salads, sandwiches, canapés—in general, the cold food items for the lunch and dinner buffets. All ice, vegetable, and fruit carvings are prepared here, as well.

"Then we have our fish, meat and poultry stations, where all preparation for these items is done individually at each station. All of our bakery products are made onboard. The bakery is in operation twenty-four hours a day."

The captain led the way to the pastry area.

"This is where all desserts and pastry items are made fresh on a daily basis," he observed. "We use more than two hundred pounds of white chocolate and three hundred pounds of dark chocolate per cruise."

"Mmm." Juliette feigned a swoon. "All that talk of chocolate is making me hungry."

"Good, because in a little while we're going to have a tray of desserts to sample," the captain promised.

Kate piped up. "You must have quite a shopping list."

"Yes. Just to give you a taste of the typical weekly supply list for our executive chef and inventory accountant, we order 3,600 pounds of butter, 1,500 pounds of pasta, 5,500 pounds of cheese, 3,900 pounds of sugar, 5,600 dozen fresh eggs, 8,700 pounds of fish—and the list goes on."

"What about ice cream?" Juliette asked.

"A thousand gallons," said the captain.

"Coffee? I could use some right about now," said Kate.

"Twenty-three hundred pounds of coffee," said the captain.

"That would keep me up." Kate yawned.

"And wine?" Jack wondered.

"One hundred and fifty different types."

"Holy mackerel, Andy."

Juliette was getting used to the Chief's antiquated colloquial expressions.

"And now I'll introduce you to our executive chef, Henri. We produce a minimum of 11,000 meals a day, breakfast, lunch and dinner, and Henri is in charge of the whole production."

"There are three chefs. Two chefs are responsible for breakfast, and we also have an executive sous chef and a butcher," said Henri. "Altogether, we have two hundred thirty-five cooks and associate cooks."

"Heavens, do they serve breakfast in bed?" Will's eyes sparkled as he gave Juliette a knowing look.

"Will," Juliette pleaded, her face coloring. The man was relentless. Tempting as it was, since she had denied herself the pleasures of a man for so long, she was not going to fall for his Romeo brand of seduction.

"Of course they do," said the captain. "Perfect for you honeymooners."

"The food staff work in ten-hour shifts, with two or three breaks a day. We have a hot section and a cold section. In the cold section, the pantry holds all the cold cuts. Sandwiches are prepared here, and canapés. Typically we operate on a seven-day cycle, but on the repositioning cruise, it's a fourteen-day cycle. In port, we'll have an on-line buffet. Also, our kitchen is electric only. We don't use any gas," explained Henri. "On a typical cruise we might have eight hundred or more children, and they eat chicken nuggets and hotdogs, but there are not as many kids on the repositioning cruise."

"What's the average age of the guests?" Jack asked.

"Forty-five to forty-nine, on most cruises," answered the captain. "But sixty-five to seventy on a repositioning cruise. "On a full cruise we will have 4,631 guests. But on this cruise, for example, we have 1,964 guests from the U.S., 492 from the UK, and 310 from Spain."

The captain moved on to the next room, and his entourage followed as he continued his course in *Sea Nymph* 101. Sweet scents wafted in the air.

"This is our pastry shop, the only place where we do production for the entire ship. Pastry is prepared down here for anywhere on the ship where we serve sweets. Maurice, here, is our chief pastry chef, and his assistant chief pastry chef is Marie. This is a twenty-four-hour operation; the night shift prepares pastries for breakfast."

Maurice brought out a tray and everyone helped themselves to samples. Kate snagged a miniature key lime pie, while Juliette picked up a sugary chocolate delight. Will and Jack each grabbed a nutty confection.

"Mmm," murmured Juliette. Will smoothed his

hand across her upper lip to remove some excess powdered sugar, and Juliette glowered.

Will threw up his hands in a gesture of mock apology. "Don't get your hackles up."

Juliette picked up another dessert and this time licked the sugar from her lips with her tongue before the Chief got any ideas. But that probably still gave him ideas. Anything she did or any movement she made gave the man ideas.

"The bakery shop prepares, from scratch, all the desserts needed for the day. We use a variety of different flours. We have a weighing scale, and a proofing machine for yeast."

Another trolley full of croissants, muffins, and doughnuts was wheeled out by a man garbed in a white apron and a chef's hat.

"This area is supervised by one chief baker and an assistant chief baker. We use 250 pounds of chocolate a day, 100 kilograms of sugar, a minimum of 100 dozen eggs a day, and 120 pounds of butter."

"I can feel the pounds piling on already," Kate quipped.

"You can eat as much as you want, Kate; I'll still love you. And you need to eat enough for Baby Jack."

"Jack!"

"I know, I said I'd stop talking about it, but what if—?"

"Jack, I'm not pregnant," Kate whispered.

"Yet," Jack said.

Kate and Jack stared into each other's eyes.

Juliette sighed. "It must be wonderful to be so in love." She looked at Kate, then let her eyes roam to her daughter's abdomen, and her hand flew to her heart as she felt the power of the amethyst. She smiled, her eyes holding a secret. A secret sweeter than the confections they had just sampled. A secret not even Jack or Kate knew. A secret they would soon discover together.

"Just like us," Will said, lifting Juliette's hand and kissing the back of it. "Two lovebirds."

"In love for real," hissed Juliette, who despaired of ever finding her true love.

"And it all has to be stored properly in the provision area," interrupted the captain, moving the group along. "We load the food once a week to keep it fresh. Bob is our storekeeper. He handles provisions and food detail and has twenty-one personnel under him. The overall supervisor is the provision master. He orders food and glassware for the bar, and chinaware.

"The provision master makes sure he's cleared room for everything that's needed and that there are no drugs smuggled onboard, or homemade bombs," said the captain. "He reviews the invoices and checks the cleanliness and quality of the goods. We store hard sweet watermelons, fresh limes, strawberries, bananas, berries, cantaloupe, and pineapples. We load 30,000 to 40,000 pounds of fresh fruits in port and flash freeze them, enough for seven days of consumption, and keep the temperature at minus nine degrees Fahrenheit to avoid spoiling. Then if we run out, we replenish our supply at another port, depending on which fruit is in season. We don't allow wooden pallets, only plastic, in the storeroom, to avoid contamination. Depending on the number of passengers, every day we prepare 300 to 500 pounds of fruit. We also keep meat and poultry in the freezer, as well as eggs and fresh produce, frozen apple juice, and whole fruit."

"This is all very interesting," Kate whispered to Jack, "but why do we need to know every single detail about every part of the ship? Do you think we might find a murderer among the mangoes or a killer in the kumquats?"

"That's really not as funny as you think, honey. There are unlimited places a bad guy might hide, so we need to be familiar with the inner workings of the ship and the players above board and below. Although a person could freeze in here. I remember when I was working for the Atlanta Police Department we had to know everything about the Midtown precinct. And this ship is like a floating city."

"That makes sense," agreed Kate, placing her hand over her mouth to stifle another yawn.

The captain droned on. "No matter how many stripes you have, requisitioning requires permissions. If I have a request, I give it to the executive chef and he gives it to the provision master. Oh, and we have an emergency backup generator on board to supply the freezer," the captain added, shuffling his charges along to another area.

"What's in this area marked Secret?" Juliette asked.

"This is our waste treatment area. We operate 24/7, and there are seven guys on two shifts in the garbage room. All waste on ship is processed in here. This is the third largest cruise ship in the world. With six thousand aboard, it's like a small town, but we can't get rid of the sewage until we're twelve nautical miles off land.

"We consume approximately 211,360 gallons a day of fresh water, and we're also able to produce fresh water on board from sea water through the process of evaporation and reverse osmosis," the captain explained.

"We have twenty-three stations and a food drainage system. The food goes into the main tanks and is cut with blades and turned into slurry. We feed the fish in the Mediterranean, but we do not feed the seagulls."

He then led the group to the housekeeping department. "Housekeeping cleans twice a day," said the captain, walking them through the laundry facilities while he spoke of the two tunnel-wash systems that could handle more than fourteen tons within twenty-four hours, the four wet-cleaning machines, the two dryers for the wet cleaning machines, and the nine medium washing machines.

"That's a lot of laundry," said Juliette.

The captain agreed and continued. "Our laundry master operates this shop 24-7, nonstop. There are twenty laundry personnel working three shifts. We clean napkins, towels, sheets and more; we wash and press. Yellow tags indicate clean; blue is dirty; red is special linen. We avoid cross-contamination in dry cleaning. We have two types of batch washing machines, a tumble washing machine, and a pressing machine. It's a very high-tech operation. Every two and a half minutes we load another twenty-five kilograms of dirty clothes. The dryers are automatic. The soap is automatic. We do six pieces a minute of duvet covers, 30,000 pieces of linen, 15,000 napkins, 15,000 towels, and here's the pressing area.

"The towel machine folds the towels automatically. There's a flatwork ironer for automatic folding. Then there's spa linen, which is tumbled in the washing machine."

"I'd like to have some of those machines in my house," said Juliette.

"Wouldn't everyone?" Kate laughed.

"Now we'll go up to the bridge viewing room. Everything goes through the bridge. Everything is under our control. We have all the information we need here." Once there, the captain introduced them to First Officer Alonzo Gonzales.

Will frowned as the first officer lifted Juliette's hand and kissed it.

"Where are we now?" Juliette asked the first officer.

"We're leaving Barcelona, and you can see all the sailing boats, so you have to be very careful to keep a safe distance from the traffic," he said from in front of the radar screen. "The next closest port is one nautical mile away. Here's the reporting point, the next and last ports of call, the number of crew and passengers, and the fuel gauge.

"Our automatic radar plotting aids give the navigator a picture of the coastline, islands, beacons, other ships, and similar objects on the surface. Our GPS consists of twenty-four satellites in orbit around the earth, which allows us to maintain continuous tracking of the ship's position, exact speed, and accurate time.

"Weather updates are sent four times a day, and we log our weather in progress in the log book. We write everything, but it's also communicated electronically online with the office. We know where we are, we check our wind speed, and we track the swells," he said, looking into Juliette's eyes and then letting his gaze rove farther down to settle on her breasts. "Right now, it's quite smooth."

Will grabbed Juliette's hand possessively while Alonzo spouted off about the gyro compass, the magnetic compass, the electronic navigational charts, marine navigation systems, and echo sounders.

"Our sea maps show all land, water depth, buoys, piers, and currents. And our sextant is used for celestial navigation so we can determine our position by the sun, stars, planets, and the moon."

"Impressive," said Juliette.

"Here's where we steer the ship, at the steering console. There are three ways to steer the ship— manually, on auto pilot, and with our backup. And besides these steering controls at the center cockpit, there are steering controls on each bridge wing.

"Our ballast tank is filled with sea water, so if the ship lists we can transfer the ballast from one side to another to make it upright again. We have two pumps, and it takes only two minutes to correct by computer. We wouldn't want the beautiful lady to lose her balance."

Alonzo reached out as if to catch Juliette off balance. He was flirting as though he knew her onboard marriage was a sham. Or maybe he just didn't care about traditional matrimonial boundaries. And truly, First Officer Gonzalez was very nice to look at.

"We will cancel a port if it gets really windy," continued the first officer, ignoring Will's grunts.

"How long does the crew stay on the ship?" Juliette asked.

"For the captain, it's ten weeks on and ten off," noted the first officer. "The first officer rotates every twelve weeks, and the second officer every six months.

After this cruise, I will have some free time."

"Which he will presumably spend with his wife and four children," said the captain, smiling, in an attempt to unruffle Will's feathers.

"Oh," said Juliette, sounding a little disappointed.

"I am my own man," claimed Alonzo proudly.

Will smiled and wrapped his arm around Juliette's waist.

"We try to keep the same team from cruise to cruise," noted the captain, "except for the free time rotation."

"What happens in case of emergency?" Kate asked.

"We use a signal horn and an alarm bell to sound the general emergency alarm, which is seven short blasts and one long blast.

"We have six hundred forty-eight fire hydrants and seven fire stations, with a dedicated certified firefighting team onboard, just in case. To ensure the safety of all guests, every week we hold a simulated emergency drill for crew members. We simulate fires, groundings, crash stops, man overboard. And on embarkation we hold a mandatory passenger drill to familiarize the passengers with onboard procedures in the unlikely event there is an emergency. An alarm will sound on the bridge if a detector has been activated. The panel will display the exact location of the alarm. Detectors can be activated by smoke or heat, or if removed or tampered with. Don't touch this panel."

"Do you have many emergencies?" Juliette wondered.

"More often than you would imagine," confirmed the captain. "Mostly it's someone who's had too much to drink."

"What happens in that event?"

"Well, for a man overboard, we reduce speed right away and follow emergency procedures, prepare a rescue board, and dispatch a rescue-and-medical team. We can stop the ship quite quickly, in seven minutes. We have a global maritime distress and safety system with medium and high frequency communications as well as satellite communications, which we test every day.

"We assess and evaluate emergency situations from the safety center here on the bridge with a variety of safety equipment controls and devices.

"On our last cruise, when we were in France, we had a medical emergency and had to medevac a passenger from the eighteenth deck. The chopper hovered around the ship, landed up here on the top deck, and then the crew rappelled down the side of the ship to get to the passenger and bring him back up to go on the helicopter to the nearest hospital, which was on Corsica."

"What if there was an emergency that required you to evacuate the ship?" Kate inquired.

"We have twenty lifeboats—twelve hold 293 people each, and eight tender boats hold 267 people each, for a total of 5,652 people," noted the captain. "Then we have two rescue boats, and two chute stations with nineteen life rafts, in total. Each life raft holds 158 people, so that's a total of 3,002 people. We have 13,266 life jackets. Our maximum combined lifeboat and life raft capacity is 8,654 people.

"We have six engines and can go a maximum speed of twenty-four knots," he said, speaking from around the chart table and showing the electronic chart display indicator systems.

"How deep is it here?" asked Juliette.

"Fifty meters, in the shallow depth, to 2,000 meters down," the captain answered. "There are two officers on watch at all times in the cockpit during navigation, the first officer and the second officer. They use binoculars and report to the officers of the ship. There's a lookout, an experienced seaman.

"Truthfully, the ship steers on autopilot—just follow the red line—but if the traffic or weather dictates, we can alter our course. We follow the traffic. Our bridge and Web camera shows a twenty-four-hour front view of the ship's bow. Our maneuvering panel, located on the center of the bridge, controls the operations of the main engines and bow thrusters. This allows me to look down the sides of the ship as we pull into and away from a pier. We're equipped with the most sophisticated telecommunications system available and a Navtex system that receives navigational warnings and weather forecasts."

The captain took his seat at the console in the captain's chair. "First Officer Gonzalez will take you back on deck. I know this is a lot to absorb, but for now, just familiarize yourselves with the ship, relax, and we'll have another meeting at dinner to go over the plan."

"I've never been on a cruise before," said Juliette. "Well, I came over from Europe on a ship, but it was nothing like this, not a fancy cruise ship. This ship is huge."

"It's made of seventy-seven million pounds of steel," Alonzo pointed out. "Our electrical cables would cover 1,740 miles. We have the biggest outdoor TV screen at sea—323 inches; the longest waterslides at sea; and the largest crystal LED chandelier ever designed. There are sixteen passenger elevators and fourteen service elevators for the crew.

"The ship's registry is in Nassau, Bahamas," he added, "and we have nineteen guest decks. And now, unfortunately, I must leave my most beautiful guest." He kissed Juliette's hand again, ignored Will, and inclined his head to Jack and Kate. "I hope you enjoy your cruise." He turned to Juliette. "And I hope I have the pleasure of your company again during our sailing. Perhaps at dinner at the captain's table?"

Juliette blushed. "I would like that."

Chapter Four

Juliette walked onto the balcony of her cabin and stared mindlessly out at the ocean. A large black crow settled on the railing, perching in front of her, bringing her back to reality. The crow hopped up and down. Juliette extended her hand, and the crow lighted on her arm.

Will followed her out onto the balcony and drew back when he saw her with the crow.

"Holy cow, Juliette," he shouted. "Is that a hawk?"

Juliette laughed. "No, it's a crow. He's been following us since the ship set sail."

"Isn't that bad luck or something? My mama had the sixth sense, and she always used to say, 'Where the crow flies, bad luck follows.' "

"Your mama was a smart woman, Chief Bradley," Juliette said, stroking the bird's back and cooing, "Old soul."

"Why don't you call me Will? We *are* married."

"Not legally. But, all right, Will, there's definitely something dark happening on this ship. Evil is lurking in our midst."

"My mama predicted that my wife would die an untimely death, and she did. I should have listened to her. I should have protected her, and now my sainted wife is gone."

Feeling his pain, Juliette put her hand on Will's.

"I'm sorry for your loss. But unless you killed your wife, you aren't responsible for her death."

"I should have done something."

Juliette patted the chair next to her and invited Will to sit down. He stared at the crow, hesitated, then took a seat. She turned to him. "How did she die, if you don't mind my asking?"

Will inhaled a deep breath before he spoke, and even then his voice came close to breaking. "I haven't talked about it with anyone, since I lost her."

Juliette nodded, sitting perfectly still, ready to listen.

"It was a dark and rainy night," Will began. "You couldn't see beyond the windshield—the fog was as thick as pea soup, the way it gets sometimes in Graysville. My wife was driving home from the grocery store. She went just to get my favorite dessert for dinner. She didn't see the tractor trailer that pulled out in front of her with no warning. And, like that, she was gone. As Chief, I got the call about the accident, and until I saw her car, I had no idea it was my wife I was looking at. She was the love of my life."

"I'm so sorry to hear that." Juliette placed her hand over his again.

"I still remember our last conversation. 'Honey,' I said, 'would you mind picking me up one of those cream-filled chocolate cakes they have at the grocery? I'm in the mood for something sweet.' If I hadn't asked her to pick up the cake, then maybe she'd still be alive. I should have—"

"We can't live our lives on maybes and should haves," Juliette interrupted. "What good does that do? It was just her time." She removed her hand and whispered, "How old was your wife when she died?"

"Thirty years old. We'd only been married for five years. My mama told me it wouldn't last. She was always predicting gloom and doom, and she was always right. She saw a black crow the night my wife died."

The Chief tried to swat the crow away.

"Stop that," Juliette warned. "He is not harming anyone."

"Why are you getting near that thing if it's an evil omen?"

"We're communicating," Juliette murmured, continuing to stroke the crow's back delicately. "Now why couldn't you be a swallow? Swallows at sea are a good sign."

Caa-Caa. The crow sounded off like he was trying to justify his presence to Juliette.

Juliette continued to stroke the crow calmly. "I know. You are a great big, handsome thing. And so sweet to drop by and pay me a visit."

Chief Bradley moved closer to Juliette and started to rub her back, imitating the strokes Juliette was using to pet the crow.

"That's a nice dress you have on, Juliette."

"Stop touching me, Chief Bradley," Juliette said evenly.

"I'll stop touching you if you stop calling me Chief Bradley. We're married, so you can call me by my first name."

"Like I said, we're not *really* married, Will, and stop touching me." It was obvious the Chief hadn't been with a woman in a long time. He was horny as a rhinoceros and just as clumsy.

"You touched me first," the Chief replied, tapping

his forefinger on the spot where her hand had touched his.

Juliette shrugged. "I was just trying to comfort you."

The crow fluttered, left his perch on Juliette' hand, and started to attack the Chief.

"Get him off me," Will screeched.

Juliette looked at the crow, and they came to an understanding. The crow flew off.

"I swear that crow was jealous," Will sputtered.

"A big man like you, afraid of a little crow?"

"That crow was huge. It was a killer crow."

Juliette laughed.

Will continued to massage Juliette's back.

Juliette twisted out of Will's reach.

"I told you to stop touching me."

"Then stop wearing such a sexy dress. It's giving me ideas."

Juliette rolled her eyes. She turned to face Will. "*We* need to come to an understanding, *Will*. Outside the cabin, we're man and wife, but I won't tolerate your manhandling. In case you want my advice, I don't think most women appreciate that kind of behavior."

"We're newlyweds," quipped Will.

"That's wishful thinking."

"A husband has his privileges."

"Not a fake husband. In the privacy of our own cabin, I'm off limits to you. I've had enough of men trying to control me, use me," said Juliette, shaking her head in disgust.

Will continued to rub her shoulders and neck.

"Then don't dress like you want to be *un*dressed."

"My daughter picked out this dress—my whole

wardrobe, in fact. We're on a cruise, for heaven's sake. Do you want me to dress like a monk?"

"Just don't expect me to behave like one," Will responded.

"I'm leaving now," Juliette announced, getting out of the lounge chair. "I'm meeting Jack and Kate in the bar before dinner."

Will followed her inside and locked the door to the balcony. He rummaged through Juliette's closet and found a black wool shawl, which he wrapped around her shoulders.

"Here, wear this. It can get cold on the ship in the evening."

Juliette tried her best to be gracious, but she remained cynical. "Thank you, *Will*."

Maybe the chivalrous Chief had a little Andy of Mayberry in him after all.

Chapter Five

"Juliette, we're over here."

Kate waved from a white leather couch in the bar, where she was seated next to Jack.

Juliette smiled when she saw Kate. She was so grateful for the opportunity to spend some relaxing time with her daughter, the daughter she'd been searching for and hoping to reconnect with her whole life, ever since that monster, her former lover, the Reverend Carter Coulter, had snatched her away. Thankfully, the nightmare was over. She had reconnected with her daughter after a painful separation and their lives were finally on the right path.

Juliette made her way to the couch, and Kate patted a space next to her. Jack nodded and moved to make room for Juliette.

"You know, I don't think I'll ever get over how much you two look alike," said Jack. "Where's your better half?"

"Don't even joke about that, Jack. He's still in the cabin, probably primping in front of the mirror. He said he'd join us in the bar before dinner."

"Is he behaving himself?" Kate asked, straightening her black pencil skirt.

"He's pretty much a horn dog," Juliette replied.

"I think he likes you, Juliette," Kate said.

"He has the hots for you," Jack clarified. "He told

me you were the first woman he had an interest in since his wife died."

Juliette sighed doubtfully. "I might believe that if he didn't ogle me like I was a call girl. I can tell he's the kind of man who's used to getting his own way."

"You have to admit he's a hunk," Kate said. "I mean that body, that build, that killer smile."

"I've noticed," admitted Juliette, "But I'm not interested in getting involved with another smooth operator. I don't care how good-looking he is. It's obvious he needs a woman, but it's not going to be me, just because I'm handy and he's randy."

Laughing, Kate changed the subject. "Juliette, er, Mom, have you been getting any strong feelings about our case?"

Juliette smiled. Her daughter was calling her Mom. That was a big step in their relationship. "Yes, I've been seeing signs. Omens. A black crow…"

"Oh, I saw one too."

"Did he approach you?"

"Yes, he sat on my shoulder. I wasn't afraid. I think he was trying to warn me."

"Exactly. And you, my child, have a particular sensitivity to evil. It's hereditary. The crow is a symbol of death, *imminent* death."

"What is a crow doing all the way out here in the ocean?" Jack asked. "Isn't that unusual?"

"Highly unusual," acknowledged Juliette. "But it's a sign from the universe. The spirit world. There's dark matter afloat on this ship."

"Are you talking about that big-ass crow outside our cabin?" Will interrupted, plopping down beside Juliette and surprising her with a kiss on the lips. "It almost pecked my eyes out. But it was gentle as a sparrow with my wife."

Juliette frowned. "Will, how many times do I need to tell you there's no need to pretend we're married when it's just Jack and Kate."

"Just practicing." Will flashed a dazzling smile.

Juliette sighed and glanced at Will. "You're impossible, Will Bradley."

"The girls were just talking about a death aboard ship."

"A death that's already happened?" Will asked.

"Soon," Juliette promised. "It will happen very soon."

"Should we alert the captain?" Jack asked.

"You might want to, but I don't think there's anything he can do to prevent it. It's fated. I'd like to walk around the ship before dinner, see if Kate or I get any strong feelings, or sense anything irregular."

"Then let's do it, ladies," said Will, springing up and pulling Juliette with him. Grabbing her hand, he started toward the door.

"Will," Juliette admonished.

"Just holding my wife's hand," Will said, smiling and warming her hand in both of his. "A husband's prerogative."

"What you're doing is taking advantage."

"Whenever I can," Will said, planting another sloppy kiss on Juliette's lips.

Juliette went to slap him with her free hand, and he grabbed it and brought it up to his lips.

"Everyone is looking at us now, sweetheart. Let's give them something to wag their tongues about."

Will wrapped his arms around Juliette, then bent

her back dramatically, kissing her slowly and thoroughly. He pressed himself against her, and she shivered until she felt his arousal. She tried to speak but was trapped by his strong arms and his gentle lips. She tried to fight her feelings, but, she had to admit, the Chief was making her feel something. Something monumental.

Some couples walking by clapped. The men gave Will a thumbs-up.

Finally, he let her go.

"Don't do that again," Juliette hissed, straightening the sleeve of her dress from where it had slipped off her shoulder.

"It felt good, didn't it, sugar?" Will challenged.

"Maybe to you, but not to me." Juliette colored, and she made a show of smoothing the wrinkles out of her wrinkle-free dress. She wondered if the Chief knew she was lying.

"Just let go, Juliette. You're so uptight. You know you felt something. Let's see where it takes us."

"I know where it's going to take us. Nowhere. And if you kiss me like that again, you'll be sorry."

"Now don't go getting your feathers all ruffled. What are you going to do, turn me into a frog?"

Juliette mustered up her most malevolent glare and fixed him with her cold-as-steel violet eyes. "Don't tempt me, Will Bradley. You don't want to mess with me. I killed a man, remember?"

"A man who deserved to die," Will said. "Someday, I'd like to hear the story, from you."

"Instead of the tabloids? Well, I killed him, and I'd do it again. Just mull that over, next time you decide to paw me in public," Juliette threatened.

"I wasn't pawing you. I'm trying to get through that frigid exterior of yours to the soft woman I know is inside." Will stared at Juliette's breasts. "I'm trying to show you how I feel. I'm attracted to you, Juliette. And that's the God's honest truth. I like having a wife again. I like it a lot."

Juliette bit her bottom lip and stared into Will's mind but couldn't quite read him. The man certainly sounded sincere. It's just that he was in dire need of a relationship manual. He came on like a speeding freight train.

"This is all a game to you, isn't it, Will? Well, I'm through being some man's pawn. I'm through being easy. I have to protect myself."

"You don't need protecting from me, sugar."

Juliette tightened the shawl around her shoulders. She felt feverish, then shaky. Perhaps she was coming down with something.

She walked away from Will and minutes later found herself in a room full of paintings, drawings, and prints.

"We're having our art auction at the end of the cruise," said a woman who stepped out from behind a podium. Would you care to take a look around? See if there's anything you like? Here's a brochure about the auction. We're one of the largest privately owned galleries in the world. If you see something that strikes your fancy, just find our auctioneer and he'll explain what to do."

Juliette took the brochure the woman offered. Jack and Kate stood behind her.

"Mom, are you all right?"

Juliette turned to Kate. "Do we have time before

dinner to visit the gallery?"

"Sure, I'll come with you. I studied art history in college, and I used to work in a gallery. Did you know that?"

"No, I didn't. There's a lot about you I didn't know, that I missed out on. Let's go in together."

Will and Jack stood guard outside the gallery.

"How are things going with Juliette?" Jack asked.

"I can't figure that woman out," Will said. "After my wife died, I couldn't fight the women off. I'm considered something of a ladies' man back in Graysville."

Jack smiled.

"But Juliette, well, she's the most beautiful woman I've ever seen, and the strongest. There's something going on between us. There's a spark, a fire, but she won't admit it. It happens every time I touch her. But she won't let me in."

"Will, she's been through a lot. She's been hurt. I want to make sure you're not going to hurt her again."

"I'm not like that lecherous reverend. She might be surprised, if she'd give me half a chance."

"Maybe you're coming on too strong," Jack suggested.

"I only have two weeks. Then y'all are going back to Atlanta. She won't let me near her in the cabin. The only chance I have of wearing down her resistance is in public, where I can kiss her or touch her, make a physical connection."

"But you just met her. I think things are happening too quickly for her taste. Women like to be courted."

"But every time I look at her, every time I'm around her, I go crazy. Jack, she is driving me insane."

Jack chuckled. "That's the way I felt about Kate. It was instant, like a lightning bolt."

"I'm just going to have to use the time I have with her to get her to realize we were meant for each other."

Jack shook his head. "You've got it bad, Will."

Will acknowledged that he did. "I hope the girls come back out soon. I'm getting hungry."

Chapter Six

Kate and Juliette roamed the gallery for the next half hour, impressed by the wide selection of European artists on display. They wandered into an isolated alcove of the gallery and looked through another stack of paintings.

A man hurried over.

"Ladies, I'm afraid the gallery is closed for inventory."

Juliette looked deflated. "But the woman outside said—"

"I'm afraid she was mistaken."

"Well, we were hoping to see some of these paintings," said Kate, inching her way farther into the alcove.

Juliette tightened the shawl around her shoulders. The man, regal and tall as a giant—coal dark hair and matching moustache and beard as full as a thicket, piercing blue ageless eyes, a rather appealing man, in a tailored black suit, reminiscent of a vampire, sans cape—blocked the entrance. His evil but eerily familiar presence ushered a chill into the room, sucking all the air out, leaving the atmosphere still and rancid.

"Well, all right," he sighed, relenting in a melodious and mesmerizing voice, while dismissing them with all the hospitality of a gnat. "Then take a look around, if you must. See if there are any pieces that interest you. If you identify any you'd like to know more about, come back tomorrow and talk to another one of our art auctioneers. Our auction will be held next Saturday afternoon in this same place, but until then we can place a hold on the paintings you select. Just fill out these cards with your names and cabin numbers, and we'll reserve the paintings for you."

"How does the auction work?" Juliette wanted to know. "What did you say your name was?"

The man paused and grew more irritable. "I didn't. But it's, uh, Wade. Wade Randall."

"Do you have a card?" Juliette inquired.

"No," Wade barked abruptly. "I'm currently cataloging our collection to get it ready for the auction. I need to get back to the work I was doing before I was interrupted."

"Can we find out how the process works?" Juliette pressed.

The man shifted uncomfortably, hesitating. "Well, uh, our auctioneer will display each painting in front of the room, you'll raise your card, and he'll call out the price. Then, after we've finalized the sale, we'll reserve your painting and package it and send it to your house a month or so after the cruise."

"What if someone else wants to bid on it?" Kate asked.

"Well, that's all handled in advance. The painting is yours. You will fill out the paperwork, handle payment, and we'll mail it out."

Kate continued to flip through the stack of paintings.

"Are these Picassos?" she asked.

"Good eye," Wade said, scowling. "How did you

know?"

"Well, I majored in art history in college. I'm an art lover, and my family collects—collected—art. I recognize his style, and I can see his signature on the paintings."

"Oh, of course," Wade said, his hands fluttering nervously, before they settled on his hips.

He stood in front of the paintings for a minute, until Kate elbowed her way around him to peruse the stack further. The artwork ranged from flawless landscapes to portraits. Besides the Picassos, there were Monets, Chagalls, a very nice Vermeer, an obscure Jan van Eyck, an "unfinished" Cézanne, even a Rembrandt—*View of the Sea of Galilee*—a fine Matisse, an Old Master—a priceless Raphael?—and, if she wasn't mistaken, a still life by van Gogh, *Vase of Poppies*. What were these gems doing on a cruise ship in the middle of the Atlantic?

Overcome, Kate's hand flew to her throat. "Are these authentic? Or are they copies?"

"Which one did you have in mind?"

"Well, this Chagall, for instance," Kate said, holding up the painting. "These colors are marvelous. I don't think I've seen this suite of his before."

"It is very beautiful, but beauty is expensive. That painting is…" Wade frowned.

"Out of my price range?" Kate smiled.

"Out of most people's price range, I imagine."

Kate studied the painting.

"Are we talking $100,000?" Kate ventured.

Wade narrowed his eyes.

"Impressive. That would be about right, Miss—"

"Crystal, Katherine Crystal, or rather, Katherine

Crystal Hale now," Kate said. "My parents owned two Chagalls, very similar to this, but, well, I believe the third in the series was stolen from the Musée National Marc Chagall in Nice some years back."

"I wouldn't know anything about that. You must be mistaken, Miss Hale. We do not trade in stolen art."

Kate pressed her lips together. "Is it for sale, Mr. Randall?"

"I'm afraid these have all been pre-sold. Can I interest you in another one of our artists? We have some beautiful landscapes you and your sister might enjoy."

"Wade," Kate began, laughing to herself. Everyone mistook Juliette for her sister. They looked very much alike, and Juliette appeared to be so young that no one would have guessed they were actually mother and daughter. "I've looked through the gallery, and most of what you have here is mediocre, and I think you know that. Beautiful, yes, but to anyone who knows anything about art, to someone with a trained eye, they're hardly collectibles. Your Chagall, on the other hand, is either a damn good reproduction or it's real, and if it is, it's been off the market for years. Do you mind me asking who purchased this particular painting?"

"We don't give out personal information about our patrons," Wade said, wringing his hands impatiently.

"Has this patron bought any more paintings on this trip?"

"I'm afraid I can't say. Now, how about one of these landscapes from a yet undiscovered but very promising young painter from Prague? If you like his work, I can give you a good price."

Wade led them over to the other side of the gallery,

Kate and Juliette reluctantly following. They passed some oil and acrylic paintings on canvas, drawings, lithographs, etchings, and engravings before Juliette stopped in front of a collection of watercolors.

"Kate, these are lovely," Juliette said.

"Yes," Kate admitted. "They are pretty scenes, but—"

Wade turned over the painting to display the price: $700. "If you'd like, I can give you another by this same artist for $300, so for $1,000 you could have two paintings to take home, including the custom frames."

"I'm afraid I couldn't afford these, Mr. Randall," Juliette said, her downcast eyes expressing her disappointment.

"Mom, if you really like these paintings, I'd love to buy them for you."

"Kate, that's very generous, but I couldn't accept them."

"Fill out your name on this card. I want to buy them both for you."

Juliette smiled. "I've never owned anything so beautiful. Thank you." Juliette couldn't stop staring at the paintings.

Wade opened a drawer and pulled out a single glossy sheet. "Here is some literature about this particular artist." He handed Juliette the artist's bio. She filled out the form with her name, address, and cabin number, and handed it to Wade.

Not to be dissuaded, Kate turned purposefully back toward the original stack of paintings, to a particular Chagall. "I'm afraid I have my heart set on this Chagall or one of these other quality pieces you're hiding in the alcove. I would be willing to exceed any current bids."

"As I've told you before, they've all been presold," Wade apologized impatiently. "We're not *hiding* anything."

"By the same mysterious buyer?" Kate wondered.

Wade was silent for a moment. "Perhaps you can take another look around, ladies, to see if there's anything else you like. We have another week until the auction, and we'll be here the entire time until then."

"I'm afraid we have dinner reservations, but thank you for your time," Kate said, backing away, almost choking on the murky aura in the alcove.

"Since you're buying the paintings, you'll need to fill out a form, too," said Wade, "with your cabin number."

Juliette flashed wary eyes at the man.

The man addressed Kate, but his eyes skewered Juliette. "Miss Hale, isn't it? And what did you say your cabin number was?"

"She didn't," answered Juliette, grabbing Kate's hand as she shoved her daughter out the door, where they bumped into Jack and Will.

"Kate, what's wrong?" Jack asked. "You look as if you've seen a ghost."

"Well, in a way I have. The ghosts of some long dead artists, whose genius has survived."

"I don't understand."

"Some of the paintings Juliette and I saw in there… They're stolen. They offer those Old Masters and others as a come-on. The auctioneer claims they're all spoken for. I doubt they were ever really for sale."

"Are you sure?" Jack asked.

"Absolutely. I've not only studied these paintings or paintings like these, but I've seen them or very similar work by the same artists in galleries all over the world. Either these pieces are very skillful reproductions, or something's rotten in Denmark."

"Denmark?" Will asked. "I thought this was a Mediterranean cruise."

Kate laughed. "It's just an expression, Will. After dinner I want to take another look around—a closer look. Jack, I think these people are operating some kind of black market smuggling ring, and right under the nose of the cruise line. I'm coming back to the auction next Saturday night to find out the name of the person who has bought these paintings."

"Kate, don't you think that might be dangerous?" her husband said.

"Not if everything is on the up and up. Aren't we supposed to be looking for anything that seems suspicious? This is definitely suspicious. That man was nervous. He didn't like us poking around. He knows my name, and he tried to get my cabin number. It shouldn't be too hard to find. Maybe we should tell the captain what we've discovered."

"But Kate, I filled out a form. He knows my name and where I live," Juliette said, wringing her hands. "Which means he knows where you live. I knew I had a feeling about this gallery. And that man. I feel as though I've seen him before. But I just can't place where."

"Let's not alarm the captain. Why don't we go to dinner and talk about it."

"Good idea, Jack. I'm starving," said Will, before giving Juliette a hungry look.

Chapter Seven

"What is our plan of attack?" Will asked Jack as he cut into a juicy steak, releasing the excess blood to trickle into and ruin a perfect presentation of fluffy garlic mashed potatoes.

Well, you see, right there, Juliette rationalized, that's why she and Will could never be a couple. She detested the sight of raw meat, and Will had probably never eaten a salad in his life. The man had obviously skated through life on his good looks. Certainly he never traded on his social graces.

Of course, the Reverend Carter Coulter had possessed social graces to spare. He was polished, educated, smooth—and smarmy to the core. And she had fallen for him like a naïve schoolgirl, like so many other impressionable young sensitives in the Florida seaside community of Casa Spirito. Since that debacle, she had hardened her heart to every man. No one was ever going to break down her defenses again. She rarely looked back, not since she had murdered her former lover, but, on the plus side, if it hadn't been for the reverend, she wouldn't have Kate, the greatest gift in the world.

The seafood dish she'd ordered was delicious, lighter and flakier and more tender than anything she'd ever tasted. She studied Kate and Jack. Both had ordered the sea bass. They couldn't keep their eyes or their hands off each other. They existed in perfect harmony on every plane. Kate fairly glowed. Well, some of that had to do with her delicate condition. A condition Kate herself was not yet aware of. Juliette was going to be a grandmother.

Jack took a drink of water before he spoke.

"I'm glad the captain had to cancel on dinner. It gives us a chance to talk privately. From what the girls said, there's something fishy going on with this art auction business. We have to consider that the cruise line could be aware of it or at worst could be involved. We have no idea how these auctions work. They could be another way for the cruise line to make money, like their gambling concession. But we weren't brought on board to catch an art thief or muddy up the works of the ship. Our purpose is to protect the members of the European Union central bank conference while they negotiate a treaty. There's where the threat lies. The captain received a threat to the lives of the representatives. Now whether that will be a bomb or an assassin, we're not sure. But there's where we need to focus our efforts."

"I'm getting a bad feeling about that man in the gallery," Juliette objected. "I'm not so sure stealing art is all he's about."

"Okay. I'll have a talk with the captain and have him look into this person. Did you get his name?"

"He said his name was Wade Randall, but he didn't look like a Wade."

"Honey, just what does a Wade look like?" Will wondered.

"I don't know. Just not like him. For some reason, he seems familiar to me."

"There's something off about him that bears investigating," Kate agreed.

Jack threw up his hands. "Far be it from me to disagree with the two most talented and beautiful psychics I know."

"How many other psychics do you know, Jack?" Kate teased.

Jack gave her a smile. "I'll have the captain look at the passenger list and the employee roster. And I'll contact a friend of mine at the Art Loss Register or the Commission for Looted Art in Europe and some of the Lost Art Database websites that recover plundered art, to see if they have any record of stolen art of the type you saw at the gallery. I'll check with the FBI's arts crime unit and run it by Interpol to see if we get any hits. Kate, how do you think these paintings, if they're not forgeries, got onto the ship?"

"They could have been stolen right off the wall at a museum, or at an exhibition or showing of works by the artist, on loan from another museum or a private collector. Some of the paintings in the gallery are quite small, like 8 by 10 inches in size, or only centimeters. And then, too, the man could have smuggled a stolen painting on board hidden behind another painting. I'll bet if I took a closer look at one of those paintings from the artist in Prague, who knows what I would find? I think whoever reserved those paintings will have them shipped home and end up with one or more masterpieces, free and clear, undetected and unpunished."

"How do they get away with it?" Jack asked his wife.

"Most times they are stolen right out from under

large crowds, during celebrations, say, for example, the Olympics, or a Millennium celebration. The thieves are brazen. If the painting is large enough, they'll cut the art right out of the frame, roll it up, and disappear, which is a crime against culture in itself. Sometimes they will steal only a panel of an altarpiece. And there are private collectors who would pay dearly for the privilege of owning and hoarding such paintings or works of art, and the world would never have the joy of looking at them again."

"How much do you think these paintings are worth?" Will asked.

"Millions," Kate stated. "The auctioneer estimated $100,000 for just one piece, but collectively they are easily worth ten times that amount. The reward for information leading to their return can run into the millions. Stolen paintings in art heists are not uncommon, and even though they discount the price, the thieves walk away with a fortune, if they can unload them."

"Why would anyone do such a thing?" Juliette asked.

"For any number of reasons. Politics. Often there are ransom notes associated with a theft. Not to mention the thousands of paintings plundered, confiscated, or destroyed by the Nazis—650,000 works of art looted from Europe alone—only a fraction of which have been recovered or restored to their rightful owners or their descendants and heirs after the Holocaust."

Juliette fixed her eyes on Kate and took in her pallor. "Honey, is there something wrong?"

"I think I'm going to be sick," Kate gasped, getting up from her chair.

"Kate, sweetheart—" Jack said. "Are you seasick?"

"I'll tend to her, Jack," Juliette said. "This is a typical reaction she has. It's her sensitivity to evil."

Jack looked helpless.

"She'll be fine," Juliette assured.

Juliette helped Kate out of the restaurant and to the nearest restroom, where Kate flew into the stall, threw up, and flushed the toilet. When she walked out, her face was still an unearthly white.

"I-I don't know what happened," Kate said. "I must be seasick."

"You're sick, all right, but it has nothing to do with the sea. When was your last menstrual cycle?"

Kate flashed Juliette a puzzled look. "I know I've had a, I mean, I think I had one, at least I thought I'd had—" Kate paused and did the calculation. "I haven't had my cycle since before our honeymoon."

Juliette smiled. "Katherine Crystal Hale, you've just made me the happiest grandmother-to-be on earth."

"You mean I'm—"

"For a psychic, you are not doing such a good job of seeing into the future."

"But it's so soon."

"It only takes once, and the way you and Jack are together, I imagine you've had quite a bit of opportunity."

Kate blushed. "But how can I be sure?"

"I'm as sure as I can be," Juliette said. "I've known for a long time. In fact, I saw it the first time I saw you and Jack together in my shop. But let's see if we can find a pregnancy test somewhere aboard this ship, if you need less ethereal proof."

Kate and Juliette strolled hand in hand toward a

sundry shop.

"Won't Jack worry?" Kate said.

"Yes, and a little concern now and then won't hurt him. We'll just pick up the test and you can perform it at the first opportunity in your cabin."

"Jack and I are just getting to know each other."

"I had you when I was no more than seventeen. You're almost twice that. It's time. It's the right time."

Chapter Eight

When Jack, Kate, Juliette, and Will dropped by the gallery after dinner, the room was dark and the doors were locked.

"That's strange, for a place to be locked up when they should be encouraging people to browse the gallery for art," Juliette said. "I think we should find the captain."

"Don't we have reservations for the show tonight?" Will asked. "I was looking forward to hearing those singers."

"The only thing you're looking forward to is seeing the skimpy costumes of the girls in the show."

"Now, Juliette, honey," Will protested. "You don't know that. And they have nothing on you."

"Stuff it, Chief. I know your type. You're only interested in one thing."

"I'm only interested in one person, and that's you," Will objected.

"Just cut out the bull. No one can hear us. You're not impressing anyone but yourself."

"Now, kids, behave yourselves," Jack said. "Maybe that's just what we need, a little diversion. Starting tomorrow, we're going to have to be diligent and keep an eye on the monetary meeting. And we're at the theater already. Kate, you sure you feel up to a show?"

"I'm fine, Jack. Let's go in."

The four flashed their shipboard IDs and were waved through the line of people heading for the theater.

"Let's sit in the front," said Will.

"So you can see the breasts in the burlesque show better?" Juliette said.

Will put his arm around Juliette's shoulders.

"You know yours are the only breasts I'm interested in, darlin'."

Juliette blew out a breath. "That's crude. You're impossible, Will Bradley. I'm sure you're on the lookout for that cute Caroline Garrison we met on the behind-the-scenes tour."

Will stared into Juliette's eyes. "You're the only one I'm looking at. I'm not interested in the stage manager."

Juliette crossed her arms and tried to maneuver out of Will's arms.

"Trying to make your escape?" Will tightened his grip.

"I like to sit in the back so I can make my escape," Jack said, in an attempt to stop the sparring between Will and his mother-in-law.

"Let's compromise and sit in the middle," Kate reasoned.

The four took their seats halfway back from the stage and enjoyed the dancing, singing, flash, and fanfare.

Juliette was entranced. "I've never seen anything like this. I can't believe I'm here on a cruise, with all the delicious food and classy entertainment and the beautiful scenery. And earlier this evening, when I looked up at the stars, the constellations were so vibrant against the midnight sky. It's just magical."

Kate reached out to squeeze Juliette's hand. "I'm so glad you could come along. I've been looking forward to this time for us to really get to know each other better."

Tears slid from Juliette's eyes. She had been thinking the same thing. She couldn't remember a time when she'd been so happy. She couldn't believe she was sitting here, right next to the daughter she thought she'd lost forever.

"Don't cry," whispered Kate. "This is a happy occasion."

"I know. It just means a lot to hear you say that. This has been a dream come true. I've been waiting so long just to see you again, and this, well, it's beyond anything I could ever have imagined. Everything you've given me—the clothes, a home, a job, and you, my new family—it's just—"

"Juliette, Mom, it's nothing more than you deserve. All those years of separation? Well, they're over now. And we're together. I know you didn't give me up. I know you wanted me. Let's don't think about the past. Let's enjoy today and whatever the future has in store for us. I predict only good things."

"And soon we'll have something really important to celebrate," Juliette added.

"Ssshh," Kate signaled with a finger to her lips.

"What kind of plans are you two ladies hatching?" Jack wondered.

"Nothing, nothing at all," Juliette said, sitting back to enjoy the show.

Chapter Nine

The next morning while Jack and Will worked with the security people on protection duty at the banking meeting, Kate asked Juliette to meet her in her cabin and revealed she had made reservations at the spa.

"What will we do there?" Juliette asked.

"Get pampered."

"This is a week of firsts. My first cruise. My first visit to a spa. I feel like a queen. Did you run the test yet?"

"No. I wanted to wait until Jack was gone. And I wanted you here for moral support."

"Okay, but you don't need a test. I'm certain you're pregnant."

"Just humor me. I need scientific proof, not psychic suspicions."

Juliette sat on the bed while Kate removed the pregnancy test from the box before she disappeared into the bathroom.

Jack and Kate's suite was huge. It was magnificent, similar to the suite she and Will occupied. This was luxury she'd never before known.

"Everything okay in there?"

"So far," Kate called out.

Juliette opened the door to the balcony and looked out at the ocean. Everything was so calm and peaceful. She'd never seen such beauty. She wrapped her arms around herself and smiled. She'd never been this happy.

"Mom," Kate cried. "Come back in here."

Juliette turned toward her daughter. "Well?"

"Congratulations, Grandma! It's positive."

Hugging Kate, Juliette exulted, "I'm so happy for you. Jack will be over the moon. When are you going to tell him?"

"I don't think I should tell him on the trip. He'll be worried about me and he'll insist that I fly home."

"He just might. You'll know when the time is right."

"I don't know how I feel about it, though. Everything is happening so fast."

"Kate, you and Jack are going to make great parents. I'm so excited for you."

Kate sat back on the bed, her expression deflated.

"I know how you're feeling. You miss your mother. It doesn't hurt my feelings. She was your mother your entire life. She was the woman who raised you when I wasn't there. And this is something you would have wanted to share with her. It's not fair that she's gone, but I'm here, and I'll be here every step of the way."

"How did you know?"

"Kate, I feel what you're feeling. There's a strong bond between us, and with the baby on the way, our bond will only get stronger. I felt a bond with you even though I didn't know you. When Carter took you from me, stole you from my arms while I was still nursing you, I was frantic, hysterical, and he promised if I stayed with him he would tell me where you were. But he never did, and it was years, years before I found you again. All those lost years."

"And none of it was your fault," Kate said. "My father—the reverend—bears all the blame."

Juliette took Kate's hand.

"You're not alone anymore."

"We'd better get going or we'll be late for our appointment," Kate said, wiping away her tears. "And I'd better get rid of this box before Jack finds it."

Kate grabbed the test and the package and stuffed it into her purse. She closed the door to the suite, and she and Juliette took the elevator to the spa level. Before she checked in at the spa, she tossed the evidence into a wastebasket.

"We're here for our eleven o'clock appointment for manicures and pedicures," Kate announced.

"Mrs. Hale and Mrs. Bradley, Suites 1001 and 1002," said the woman at the receptionist area. "I have you down. Just go through that door, change into your robes, and someone will take you in for your treatments."

Kate smiled. "Thank you. Come on, Mom, let's go." They changed into robes and were led into the spa treatment area.

"Please select the polish color you want," the attendant said. "You two look so much alike. You must be sisters."

"We get that a lot," said Kate. "I'll take this shrimp color for my toes and this pearl shade for my nails."

Juliette was tempted to try a vibrant purple but instead she copied Kate. "I'll choose the same colors as my daughter."

Juliette dipped her feet into the warm, bubbling water. She'd never been more relaxed in her life. "This is marvelous, just amazing," she cooed.

"You're down for a sugar-and-honey scrub," the attendant said.

"Sounds wonderful," Juliette answered dreamily, as the attendant switched on the massage feature in the chair. Next to her Kate was receiving the same pampering.

"Thank you again, Kate. If had known how great this felt, I would have done it a long time ago." After a few moments, Juliette asked, "So has Jack found out anything yet from the captain about the mysterious man in the art gallery?"

"He left a message for the captain, and I think he should have some news soon."

"Do you hear bells?" Juliette asked.

Kate listened. "Yes, it sounds like church bells. I think it's on the sound system we have in here."

"Church bells heard at sea mean someone on the ship will die," Juliette said.

The women chatted about other matters while an attendant worked on their nails.

After their nails were dried, they went into the salon for a shampoo and blowout.

Kate looked at her mother. "Juliette, look in the mirror. You look absolutely amazing. Will is going to be drooling all over himself."

"I'm not doing this for Will. I'm doing this for myself." Juliette smiled when she saw her image reflected in the mirror.

"Well, whatever the reason, you look great. You'll be fighting off the men."

Kate wound her arm through Juliette's, and they went to the Lido deck to sit in the sun.

As they lay there, Juliette commented, "This is so

restful. I've never felt like this before."

"I'm so happy we could be here together," Kate replied.

Jack and Will strode by, and Will did a double-take.

"Holy smokes, Juliette! You look—you look like a movie star."

Juliette smiled and waited for the smart remarks, but they didn't come.

"Seriously, you look great. Would you like to take a stroll around the deck with me?"

"I don't think I can move from this spot. I am so relaxed."

"Then I'll join you."

"Kate, you look beautiful," Jack said, sliding a chair next to her lounge. "You must have had a good morning."

"We did. We treated ourselves to manicures and pedicures, had a shampoo and blowout, and now we're sunning ourselves like seals. I feel boneless. How about you?"

"We spent the day in boring meetings where absolutely nothing happened and nothing got resolved, and there are more security people in that room than conferees. I think that warning must have been a hoax. We searched everywhere for bombs, for signs of anything suspicious, and couldn't find a thing."

"Did you find out anything about the man in the gallery?"

"As a matter of fact, I did. The captain has no record of anyone by the name of Wade Randall on his crew or working with the gallery, and he doesn't fit the description of anyone who works there. The gallery is independently run, but they did a check, and they can't explain what that man was doing there."

Juliette sat up in her chair. "I'm getting a bad feeling about him."

Jack's walkie-talkie crackled.

"That was the captain. He wants to see us outside the gallery right away. Something's come up."

Chapter Ten

"They found him in the gallery storage room, covered in a tarp," whispered the captain. "He's been stabbed to death."

Kate and Juliette exchanged glances. The church bells had tolled disaster.

"How long do you think he's been there?" Jack asked.

"Well, we just set sail yesterday, but we're going to need our doctor to get more definitive information. We'll have a helicopter pick up the corpse. I want Kate and Juliette to look at the body and see if that's the man they spoke to."

Two officers escorted Kate and Juliette to the back room, where they unwrapped the tarp so the women could get a closer look at the body.

Juliette held her nose.

Kate stared at the corpse.

"T-that's not him. He doesn't look at all like Wade Randall or whoever the man we talked to really is. I think I'm going to be sick."

Juliette grabbed Kate's hand and led her out of the gallery.

"Kate," Jack called frantically when he got a look at his wife's pale face.

"She's fine. She'll be fine, Jack. I'll look after her."

"Murder seems to follow us wherever we go," Kate

said.

"Well, we are in the business of investigating murders."

"Do you think the man we met did this?"

"I don't think it was a coincidence. You could almost sense the evil emanating from the recesses of his mind."

When Kate got to the restroom, she threw up in the toilet, then stood at the sink while she washed her face.

"Feeling better?" Juliette asked, handing her a paper towel to wipe her hands.

"I'm fine. It's just seeing that body—"

"I think it was the combination of the body and the baby," Juliette said.

"We'd better get back. Jack will be worried."

The women walked back into the gallery, where Jack placed his hand on Kate's shoulder. "Are you okay, honey?"

"I'm fine," she assured Jack, looking up into eyes that reflected concern and love. "I would like to get another look at those fabulous paintings we saw last night," Kate said, as she strode over to the alcove where she and Juliette had last seen the masterpieces.

"They're gone."

"What do you mean?" asked the captain.

"The paintings that man showed us. They're gone."

Kate walked up and down the gallery aisles, looking at the walls and the prints encased in plastic.

"They were here last night, an assortment of what I think—no, what I *know,* is stolen art," Kate insisted. "Irreplaceable art."

The captain brought to Kate a man she'd never seen before. "Katherine Crystal Hale, I'd like to introduce you to the shipboard gallery manager, Pierre Dumas."

Kate stared at a plump but well-appointed gentleman who offered her his fleshy hand.

"Mrs. Hale, it's a pleasure to meet you."

Kate extended her hand. "And this is my mother, Juliette, um, Bradley."

"Mrs. Bradley," said Monsieur Pierre Dumas, inclining his head in greeting.

"Mrs. Hale says that she and her mother were speaking to an art auctioneer, who called himself Wade Randall, inside this gallery at around eight p.m. last evening. He showed them around, spoke to them about some artists, and said he was inventorying some paintings. The ladies got a look at those paintings, and from the description, they were of some import."

"They were priceless pieces," Kate interjected. "Rembrandts, Monets, a Matisse, a Vermeer, a Jan van Eyck, a Cezanne, even a van Gogh."

Monsieur Dumas laughed heartily.

"Mrs. Hale, I think you must be mistaken. We don't have the caliber of paintings you're talking about anywhere in this gallery, not on our cruise ship. We do have beautiful lithographs in color, hand signed and numbered, and an archived Old Masters' collection with original Picassos, Rembrandts, Matisses, Renoirs, Dalis, and Chagalls of impeccable provenance, as well as post-impressionists, at our U.S. gallery. But we don't offer those on the cruises. However, I assure you we maintain the highest professional standards to give passengers a premier collecting experience. Our stateside pieces come directly from the estates of deceased artists or are purchased from reputable international auction companies. But to bring those aboard ship? The insurance alone would be cost-prohibitive.

"Although there are some upscale passengers aboard, none of them could even hope to afford paintings such as those," Monsieur Dumas continued. "Ah, would I love to have even one of those works in our onboard gallery? Of course. Those priceless pieces remain locked up in our vault in the States.

"Most of our collection comes directly from living artists doing contemporary paintings of landscapes, places they've lived or visited. But our artists are primarily unknown—of a certain quality, yes, but not the equal of any of the masters you describe. The people who come to our auction here like the look of a painting that might suit the décor in their living room or dining room. They are gambling that one day, perhaps, these unknown artists will rise to the level of a Chagall and that their investment will be worth something. And that has certainly happened with many of our artists.

"We offer watercolors, giclées in color on canvas with hand embellishments, some oils on canvas. We try to demystify art by making it accessible to the passengers on cruise ship auctions. At best, we might have a Picasso print or lithograph, but for the most part, I'm afraid the level of the art we offer does not rise to the level of art auctioned off at a Christie's or a Sotheby's. We try to offer passengers something they can take home, a memento of their cruise, but no, the artworks you are talking about would never be sold on this ship."

"But I saw them," insisted Kate when she was finally able to interrupt the flow of Monsieur Dumas' monologue. "Not only did they look authentic, but many I recognized as stolen from various museums around Europe."

"And you would recognize these how?" asked Monsieur Dumas, raising his eyebrows in doubt.

Jack defended his wife. "Kate majored in art history at one of the finest colleges in the country. She's worked in a gallery. She knows about art. Her family owns a number of paintings by the artists you spoke of."

"My dear," said Monsieur Dumas. "Let us have a look around my humble gallery, and you can see for yourself that you're mistaken."

Kate spewed a stream of fluent French, and Monsieur Dumas's face colored.

"I certainly didn't mean to be condescending, Mrs. Hale. "It's just that what you say happened could not have happened, not here, not in my gallery."

"Are you calling my mother and me liars?" Kate railed. "Because we know what we saw. So if you do not carry such pieces in your gallery, then that man brought them in here, perhaps to hide while the ship is in progress, and plans to offload them when we dock or to claim them later. Is it possible that he hid them in the same frames as some of your other paintings, which he will purchase and have shipped to his house?"

Now she had Monsieur Dumas's undivided attention.

"What happens to the paintings once they leave here?" Kate demanded.

"They are sent to our facility in New York that acts as our distribution center servicing our cruise ship auctions. There the paintings are custom-framed and shipped worldwide to the buyers."

"So couldn't someone hide a masterpiece in the frame of one of your less spectacular paintings and have it ultimately shipped to his or her home?"

"I hadn't considered that, but I will check that possibility immediately."

The gallery manager went from painting to painting, checking the backs, undoing the frames, working furiously, on a mission to recheck his entire inventory.

"I will also see if anyone expressed an interest in a number of paintings to be finalized at auction next week," he added.

"Meanwhile, Kate and Juliette, I want you to come up to Security and have a look at every passenger's photo ID to see if you can help identify this mystery man," said the captain. "No one, including me, can get aboard or off the ship without showing his ID."

"Captain, I just had a thought. My wife and her mother are the only ones aboard who can identify this man. If he is the one responsible for killing the gallery employee, then we have a killer and a highly skilled art thief aboard this ship. I don't think my wife or Mrs. Bradley is safe."

"I have to agree with you," acknowledged the captain. "We aren't making a stop until we get to Bermuda. For the next few days, we'll be at sea. You will need to keep the women close at all times unless I am with them. Meanwhile, I'll have my security people gather some evidence. We'll have to do a thorough search of the ship, to see where these masterpieces are being hidden, if they are indeed aboard ship. If we determine the cabin of the man in the gallery, we can search it while he's out. If not, we'll turn this ship upside down to find him. As you saw on our tour, there are hundreds of places a person or the paintings could be hidden, especially if he has an accomplice in the crew. I'm sure the killer must have been blindsided, caught in the act by this poor gallery employee, so he will have to come up with another plan to hide the paintings. We need to stay one step ahead of him. After the body is flown off the ship and returned to Barcelona, the medical examiner and proper authorities will see if we can get an ID of the killer from DNA or fingerprints that we can circulate to Interpol and the CIA."

"What a shame the deceased discovered what Wade Randall was up to," Juliette reasoned. "He paid the price with his life."

"Kate, Juliette, why don't you go with the captain to the security area and see if you can identify this passenger," said Jack. He whispered to Will, "I don't want either of them out of your sight for one minute."

"Don't worry, Juliette, I will protect you," Will said, within earshot of the captain, kissing her cheek.

Juliette pursed her lips, trying not to react. It was almost a sweet kiss. Romantic. Protective. But there must be an underlying motive. There always was, with men like Will. He was just showing off to the captain, in front of witnesses. His tenderness toward her was anything but genuine. She was a psychic. Wouldn't she know that? Or were her growing feelings toward Will blinding her to his motives? Would she ever learn to trust a man again?

Juliette, Kate, and Will took the elevator with the captain, down to the level where the security area was located. He led them over to some monitors and assigned a crew member to pull up pictures of everyone aboard ship, both crew and passengers.

"You can sit here and look through the photos and keep advancing until you think you have a hit. We will split the photos between the two of you. If Wade Randall or the man calling himself Wade Randall is on this ship, then he's in this database, and we'll find him."

Chapter Eleven

Kate stood up from the desk, massaging her back. "I need a bathroom break. My bladder must be the size of a pea."

"Pregnancy will do that to you," Juliette whispered. "I'll come with you."

Will stood up from where he was sitting with the captain.

"Have you found something?"

"No," Juliette said. "We're taking a break."

"I'll go with you."

"You can't go where we're going," Juliette said, frowning at Will. "We're going to the ladies' room."

"But Jack gave me strict instructions not to let you out of my sight."

"I don't think he meant that literally. We've been at this for hours. We need to stretch and powder our noses."

Will came over to Juliette.

"Well, then, I'll just wait outside the door."

"Suit yourself." She and Kate headed outside the security area toward the closest restroom. Will followed.

"That man is going to drive me insane," said Juliette when they got inside.

"What's he doing?"

"He's hovering over me. And he tries to take

liberties every chance he gets."

Kate laughed. "I think he likes you, Juliette. After all, you two *are* married."

"You think this is funny? I have to sleep with the man, well, not literally, but I have to wake up beside him every morning. And his hands are always in places they shouldn't be."

"Maybe he makes you uncomfortable because you like him?"

"I most certainly do not. He's an oaf and a boor and we have nothing in common. He doesn't know the proper way to treat a lady."

"He's pretty hot."

Juliette sighed. "That's what makes this so difficult. If he wasn't so damned cute, with that sexy Southern accent, and all those muscles, and those infernal dimples... But his attentions are all an act he puts on. When we're alone, he spends most of the time trying to get into my pants."

Kate tried to smother another laugh.

"I hear you trying not to snicker in there. You are legitimately in love with your husband. I am just pretending."

"It's just that I don't think this is a proper conversation to be having with my mother. Maybe you should just try relaxing and see what happens."

"You mean you want me to actually sleep with him—for the good of the case?"

Kate came out of the stall and washed and dried her hands. "No, but try going along, and see how it makes you feel. Stop fighting him and take it from there. Let your guard down."

"Last time I did that, I fell under the spell of an evil

man."

"But you're much stronger now. And Chief Bradley is anything but evil. Besides, you're a powerful psychic. Can't you look into his mind and sense what he's feeling?"

"Can you do that with Jack?"

"Well, no, I've never been able to."

"It's just as well."

"Are you afraid of what you'll find? Maybe he really does care for you."

"And maybe he's trying to take advantage. Because, I swear, if he paws me one more time, I'm going to turn him into a—"

Kate laughed. "Come on, you can't really do that, can you?"

"I'm not a witch. But I could make him very uncomfortable in a number of delicious ways."

Juliette smiled. "What kind of mischief are you planning, Mom?"

"It's best you don't know."

The women linked arms, opened the door of the ladies' room, and nearly knocked the Chief over.

"Was everything okay in there?" he asked.

"Do you want a detailed report?" Juliette asked, her eyes twinkling.

"I just meant I wanted to make sure nothing happened."

"No art thieves or murderers lurking in the toilet, if that's what you mean."

"Juliette, you're not taking your predicament seriously. You and your daughter are the only ones who can identify that man, and he knows that, and he is somewhere on this ship. If he killed once, he will kill again."

Was that genuine concern in Will's eyes? Or was she misreading him? He was walking ahead of them, which gave her a good view of his seriously fine backside and left her wondering what it would feel like to have her hands on him and his on her. Or what it might be like to have him inside of her.

Juliette dismissed her naughty thoughts and sat down next to Kate again for another round of photo ID viewing. She doubted the man would be sloppy enough to show his true self in a passenger photo. The face of the man they had seen in the gallery was real. But she suspected he was smart enough to disguise his looks for the ID photo.

Will huddled with the captain, and then Jack came in, and the three men were deep in conversation. Jack looked over at Kate and smiled, and, sensing his presence, she looked up and returned the smile, her upturned lips an open invitation.

"I think the girls need a break," said Jack. "They've been at it most of the night and all morning. Do you mind if we take them out on the deck to get a little sun?"

"No, we have more than enough coverage on the banking meetings. Nothing seems to be happening there. We'll resume our watch this afternoon."

Jack helped Kate up from her seat and kissed her forehead.

"You look tired, honey."

"I've been staring at faces on a computer screen for an eternity."

"Well, let's take a break in the cabin, get your bathing suit, and then we'll meet Will and Juliette out on deck. Maybe we'll take a dip in the pool, grab some lunch."

"That sounds blissful," Kate sighed, hugging Jack.

"What was that for?"

"Oh, just because," Kate said.

They rode up in the elevator with Will and Juliette. Will was restraining himself, making an obvious attempt to keep his distance from Juliette. Maybe he actually believed she could turn him into a—well, a frog or something worse—with her magical talents.

Jack opened the door of their suite, and they watched as Will and Juliette entered their cabin.

"Will's got it bad for your mother."

"Do you think?"

"I know. He told me so. She's a lot of woman to handle, but Will is determined to wear her down."

"If she doesn't turn him into a frog first," Kate said.

"You're not serious."

"My mother is a very powerful psychic. There are no limits to what she could do."

"She hasn't taught you any of her tricks, has she?"

"We've been training together, but we haven't gotten to transformations yet."

"Good, because I sort of like this body."

"I like it too, very much," said Kate, winding her arms around Jack's neck.

Jack touched his head to Kate's.

"Feeling frisky?" Jack whispered.

"Always," Kate said, shuddering. "I missed you."

"I missed you too, baby. Why don't we take full advantage of this time alone?"

"What exactly did you have in mind, husband?"

Jack walked Kate backwards and gently pushed her back onto the bed. He jumped in next to her.

"It starts with the fact that you're wearing too many clothes," he said, slowly undressing Kate and removing his own clothes.

When she was naked, Jack moved his hands down her body, lingering on her breasts, her tummy, and then driving her wild with his fingers.

"Oh, Jack, don't stop, please. That feels... amazing."

Jack kept up the tension, licking her breasts, teasing her lips until she was panting with desire, taking shallow breaths. When she was about to go mad, he slipped into her and held on until they climaxed.

Jack moved to Kate's side and let out a breath. "Kate, being with you just keeps getting better and better."

Kate relaxed, stretched her arms and legs, and sighed in satisfaction.

"You're purring like a kitten," Jack said, tracing his fingers over her body, skimming her breasts and her stomach. His hands paused on her bare midriff and he sat up suddenly.

"Kate."

Kate's mouth turned up.

"Katherine Crystal Hale, is there something you'd like to tell me?"

Kate kept quiet and swallowed a smile.

"Are you...are we...Kate?" Jack stared at her.

"Yes, Daddy."

"Oh, my God, I knew it. How did it happen?"

"I think you know how it happened."

"I mean, when? How far along are you?"

"I think it happened on our honeymoon, but I haven't seen a doctor yet. I took a pregnancy test with Juliette."

"With Juliette. When did you know?"

"Last night. After I got sick."

"I thought that was seasickness."

"So did I, but Juliette knew. She's known for a while. She says she saw a vision when we were together in Casa Spirito."

Jack wrapped his arms around her and hugged her.

"I didn't hurt you, did I? Before, I mean?"

"No, of course not."

Jack paced the cabin, his voice was full of energy. "Kate, I am thrilled. How do you feel about it?"

"I was shocked, at first. It's happened so soon. But I'm getting used to the idea."

"Honey," said Jack, planting a loud kiss on her mouth and hugging her again. "I couldn't be happier. I can't wait to tell my mother. Do you think Juliette knows if it's a boy or a girl?"

"I wouldn't be surprised, but I don't want to find out that way."

"Okay, we'll find out the regular way. Have you been getting any feelings at all? Did you know?"

"No. I thought I was seasick, too."

"Do you think our baby will be psychic?"

"It's possible. It runs in the family. We'd better prepare ourselves."

Chapter Twelve

Juliette and Will dined at the outdoor café on the pool deck. From their vantage point, they observed the medevac helicopter from Barcelona hovering over the deck. The ship's physician and the captain and a small contingent of the crew had fastened the body, wrapped like a mummy in a white sheet, to the waiting winch while it was raised into the medevac. The wind whipped up furiously around the copter, twisting the cargo. Juliette wrapped a shawl around her shoulders to ward off the chill, both physical and cosmic.

"I thought bodies aboard ship were supposed to be buried at sea," said Juliette.

"Normally, yes, since we're so far out in the ocean. But in this case, since the man was murdered, the captain is sending the body back to the mainland for further investigation. We're too far out to sea to turn around."

The helicopter circled back, and Juliette watched it until it was nothing more than a black speck in the sky.

"The crew is growing restless," Will said, finishing his sandwich. "They're spooked about the death threat to the European Union banking conference, and then the murder, although we've tried to keep it a secret. But the crew knows, and now anyone out on deck can see it. The news will spread like wildfire. And a murderer is loose on the ship. All bad signs. The crew is convinced

77

this cruise is jinxed, cursed. Isn't there something you can do? Some kind of spell you can weave, or a ritual you can perform?"

"Will, I'm not a magician or a witch. The truth is, this cruise *is* cursed. The crow we saw earlier was on the railing when I woke up this morning."

"Crowzilla was back?" Will piped up.

"Yes, and with his two brothers," Juliette added. "There were three of them, all in a row. It's a classic sign. I did do a protective spell, but I'm not sure it will cover us out at sea."

"Is that why you lit all those candles in the cabin?"

"Yes."

"I thought maybe you were trying to send me a message by setting a romantic mood, but then you acted like you didn't want to be around me, as usual."

"This has nothing to do with you, Will Bradley. The world doesn't revolve around you."

"I've been on my best behavior, in case you haven't noticed."

"I've noticed." Juliette's mouth curved, and she barely hid a smile. "You're becoming more... tolerable."

"You're a tough woman. I've never had so much trouble getting a woman to warm to me. I thought maybe I'd have to handcuff you to the bed with these." Will brought out a pair of silver handcuffs from his back pocket and jangled them in front of her.

"Don't be a cretin." Juliette started to push them away and then she pulled them back and examined them more closely. "Are these real silver? They're really beautiful and shiny."

Will straightened and took them out of Juliette's

hands. "Yes. My deputies gave them to me on my fifteen-year anniversary with the force. They're not regulation, but they work. They must have set the guys back a pretty penny. I always carry them with me. They're my good-luck charm."

"Well, your charm doesn't work with me, Will Bradley."

"Not even a little?" Will smiled and flashed his dimples.

Juliette shook her head. "We have more important things to worry about than your sex appeal or lack of appeal to women."

"You think I'm sexy?" Will coaxed.

"I know you're as conceited as a peacock."

Will held up the handcuffs. "We can always take these babies out for a test drive, whenever you're ready."

"I'm not into hanky panky, Will Bradley."

"You're no fun." Will laughed good-naturedly and placed the cuffs in his back pants pocket.

Juliette took out a velvet pouch and emptied some smooth stones onto the table.

"What are those? Magic rocks?"

"In a way. They're healing stones. They have healing properties," Juliette said, as she lifted each one in turn. "This amethyst releases tension and stress. The carnelian stimulates vitality and metabolic energy. The rose quartz strengthens the heart and lungs. And the sodalite blocks radiation and negative energies. Each of them have other properties, as well, for specific physical conditions."

Juliette pulled out another pouch.

"What's in there?"

"These are pure energy rock quartz crystals used to amplify energy. Rock quartz absorbs, stores, and regulates energy. It's a master healer for any condition. The crystals work on a number of levels, and I can tune them to help attract what I desire in life."

"And what is that? I know it's not me."

"Well, I can tune them to the specific quality I want to attract in life, whether it be love, prosperity, inner peace, health, travel, creativity, or body image."

"You don't need any help in that department."

"It's not *your* image of my body I'm concerned about. I'm making a broad appeal to the universe for the safe passage of this ship."

"Well, I think it's a little too late for that dead man in the helicopter."

"I'm afraid so," Juliette admitted. She held the crystals up to the sunlight.

"Sunlight restores their energy."

Then she held them in her hand, rolling them quickly back and forth.

"This activates the crystals' personal connection with me."

"Maybe I need some of those crystals so I can improve our personal connection."

"If you want to win a woman, you don't do it by sorcery, although there are love spells."

"Well, then, how do I get through to you?"

Juliette looked at Will and pursed her lips.

"By being genuine. Just be yourself, Will, if that's even possible."

Juliette gathered her stones and crystals and replaced them in her handbag. They got up from the table and strolled around the ship.

"Let's sit here," Juliette said. "The sun is so warm here. We can hear the music by the pool, and I want to get one of those fancy drinks with an umbrella."

Will flagged down a woman with a notepad.

"Miss, we'll take two of those piña coladas with the fancy umbrellas." He gave her their cabin number, and she was on her way.

As they passed the cabana station, Will grabbed two thick cornflower blue towels engraved with *Sea Nymph* and the cruise line logo, and when they had decided on where to sit he spread them out on the wooden deck lounges.

Juliette settled in and sighed.

"This is absolute heaven," she said.

"Jack and Kate will be down in a minute," Will said.

Juliette closed her eyes, and Will adjusted the angle of his lounge and took Juliette's hand.

"Just for show," Will said.

Juliette relaxed her shoulder.

"What's wrong?" Will demanded.

"Nothing," Juliette said.

"I'm holding your hand."

"So you are," she responded.

"Why aren't you snipping at me or pulling your hand away or casting a spell?"

"Because I am so happy right now. I feel like I'm floating, and nothing can change my mood, not even you."

Will smiled and tightened his grip. No reaction.

"Juliette?" he whispered.

Juliette looked over at Will, eager to hear what he was about to say.

"Can you tell me about him, about the Reverend Carter Coulter?"

Juliette looked out at the ocean and sighed. Another voyeur interested in the prurient details of the murder. Would it ever end? Would she always be known as the girl who had an affair with the cult leader of Casa Spirito and later murdered him in cold blood in his bed and blew apart his secret society of psychics?

Will took her chin gently in his hands and twisted her face toward him until they were eye to eye. "Can you look at me when you tell it? You can trust me, Juliette."

As she read his soul, she thought she could.

"I'm sure you've read all about it in the papers."

"And I know you can't believe everything you read in the papers. I would like to hear your side."

"I can imagine what you think of me. How weak I must have been to stay with a man like that. A cult leader who preyed upon innocent young women, who got me pregnant and then stole my child. And still I stayed with him."

"You must have had a reason."

"I fancied myself in love with Carter Coulter, at first," Juliette admitted. "To me, he was like a god. He was in total control of everything and everyone in Casa Spirito. He must have had us in a trance, because we would have followed him anywhere, done anything for him. I did everything for him."

"You were only seventeen when you met, isn't that right?"

"Yes, and he was the first man I'd ever been with. He took me in. He was kind to me. He set me up in my own shop, gave me an opportunity to make a living as a psychic and a spiritual healer and a medium. He said he loved me, that I was his soulmate, that we were destined to be together, and that he was ready to leave his wife. But of course, that was what he had told all the girls he seduced. So many innocent, wayward girls. We were all strays, sensitives he took in and kept under his spell. What I didn't know was that while he was sleeping with me, he was also sleeping with all the other girls who came into town lost and looking for spiritual guidance. He used me, seduced me. He said I couldn't survive without him. That he was the leader of the church and of the community, and that he was my master."

Will grimaced but took Juliette's hand, encouraging her to continue. "Go on."

Juliette closed her eyes and remembered. "And then, I got pregnant. And I carried the baby to term. I wanted to keep the baby, but Carter had other ideas. He told me that if anyone found out the baby was his, he would lose everything. Broken trust, I think he called it. But he was more interested in maintaining control of the finances of the Casa Spirito church, money that he skimmed from church funds that only I knew about.

"I wanted to keep the baby. She was a girl. He tried to convince me to give her up. He told me we could go back to the way we were and no one would have to know. He threatened me, but once the baby was in my arms, I wouldn't let her go. I couldn't. I had already fallen in love with her.

"One night, while I was nursing the baby, he came in, had some of his disciples hold me down, and he stole her, right out of my arms. I screamed and I struggled. I screamed so loudly, but he slapped me across the face until I bled and said if I ever told anyone I would be sorry. He said if I didn't cooperate, I'd never see my baby again. But if I was a good girl, he would eventually tell me where she was. Of course, he never did. Because he had sold her to a wealthy couple in Atlanta, and I never would have found her again if Kate and Jack hadn't come looking for me."

Will clasped Juliette's hand tighter.

"Did you, were you—"

"You mean was I ever intimate again with him?"

Will nodded.

"I warmed his bed on occasion, over the years, pretended to have feelings for him, to see if I could get him to tell me where my daughter was, but once I realized he was never going to tell me, I wouldn't let him touch me again. But he wanted to. He tried everything he could to coax me back into his bed over the years. But I refused to fall for his lies and false promises. And I stayed because I had nowhere else to go. Casa Spirito was my home. And because I hoped one day he'd tell me where to find my daughter. And because he continued to do the same thing to so many other girls, and I stayed to help them."

A quiet stream of tears flowed from Juliette's eyes.

Will wiped away the tears with his thumb.

"You were just a child. He was twice your age. He took advantage. He murdered Kate's parents."

"And when Kate told me who she was and what had happened to her parents, I knew Carter was serious when he said he would kill her if she exposed him. He trapped Kate and Jack in his house, drugged Kate, and had her in his bed, about to rape her. He called it trance sex. He used the same words and the same technique on me. 'No inhibitions,' he said. 'Once I put you under, you will stop struggling, and I will take you to levels you've never dreamed of.' Carter loved a good struggle. He told Kate he would be her spiritual guide and that theirs would be a perfect union. She, his own daughter, was created in his image, and his lifeblood flowed through her veins, and with her psychic ability and his superior talent, the children that would spring from their loins would be magnificent. His vision was to propagate his own stable of psychics, with Kate as his brood mare. He called it fulfilling their destiny. Carter would have killed Jack next. So I killed him first."

"You were justified, Juliette. As the chief of police, I would have done the same thing. I only wish I had killed the bastard first."

"You didn't even know me then, Will."

"But I do now. And I know you're a good person. And you are a good mother to Kate. You can tell how much she loves you."

Juliette licked some stray tears from her lips. "Thank you, Will. I was so ashamed."

"You have no reason to be, not with me." Will leaned in and hugged Juliette, who heaved a heavy sigh, leaned back on the lounge chair, and drifted off to sleep. Will placed Juliette's wide-brimmed yellow straw hat loosely over her face. Then he took her hand and wouldn't let go.

"Will, buddy, there you are." Jack ambled over, pushed two lounge chairs together next to Juliette's chair, and covered them with blue signature cruise ship towels.

"Mind if we join you?" Jack asked. He and Kate settled on their chairs, staring out at the ocean. "What's wrong with Juliette?"

"Juliette?" Will whispered. "Juliette?"

"She's asleep," Kate observed. "She must be exhausted."

Will dropped Juliette's hand.

"I guess that's why she didn't get mad when I grabbed her hand. She was too tired to care."

Kate stifled a giggle.

"Give her time, Will. You're just getting to know each other. You never know what surprises are in store."

Jack and Kate looked at each other and grinned.

"What's with you two?"

"Nothing," Jack said smiling.

"Nope," Kate mimicked. "Not a thing."

"I'll be glad when we dock in Bermuda," Will said. "I'm getting antsy on this ship."

"I'm enjoying these days at sea," murmured Juliette. "So peaceful. I've never been to Bermuda, Will, have you?"

Will turned toward Juliette, "You're awake. No, my wife and I never traveled much. She was pretty much a homebody. I feel like I'm starting over, like I've been given a second chance."

"Jack and Kate spent their honeymoon in Bermuda. They're looking forward to showing us around. I can't wait to do some shopping."

"Is it true that the sand in Bermuda is pink?" Will wondered.

"Absolutely," said Kate. "And they have some of the best beaches in the world, surrounded by turquoise waters. And the houses are so colorful, painted in sea greens and sky blues, yellows, and lilacs."

"I'm ready for some adventure," Will admitted.

"Murder isn't adventurous enough for you?" Juliette snickered.

"There's lots to do there," said Kate. "When we dock, we should rent motorcycles and ride around the island. And most people don't know this, but Bermuda is actually comprised of a hundred and eighty-one islands, islets, and rocks. Or we can go horseback riding. And Jack and I know some great restaurants. We're going to be there two days, so we'll definitely want to go to the beach. Bermuda is a shipwreck-diving capital, and there's more golf per square mile than anywhere else in the world. There are some great water sports, like sailing, windsurfing, water skiing, body surfing, snorkeling, deep-sea fishing, kayaking, windsurfing, and swimming with dolphins."

"We haven't seen a porpoise, a dolphin, or sea life of any kind out here yet," Will remarked, "except for those super-sized crows of yours."

"They're not *my* crows," mumbled Juliette under her floppy sun hat.

"The one I saw seemed pretty attached to you."

Two women ambled by in walkers.

"Unless you count those women walking at a turtle's pace, but not a sea turtle."

"That's not very nice, Will," Juliette chided. "But you're right. We haven't seen a dolphin, and dolphins swimming with the ship are a sign of good luck. But I did see a shark following the ship. That's a sure sign of inevitable death."

Will shuddered. "Have you noticed that the average age on this boat is a hundred and six? I've only seen one cute honey so far, and that's you," Will continued. "And of course, you, Kate."

"Keep that up, and I'll turn you into a sea turtle. You know we're not on this cruise for our enjoyment. This is an assignment. So far no one has been able to turn up any leads by conventional means. So Kate and I are going to have to resort to some psychic solutions."

Chapter Thirteen

"Kate and I spent almost the entire morning cooped up in the security office looking at the rest of the ID shots, and neither of us could identify anyone who resembled the art thief," Juliette said, as the two couples sat down to lunch in the main dining room. "He should be easy enough to spot on the ship, he's so tall. And that beard is so distinctive. But he's laying low, either in the crew quarters or in one of the guest rooms. I hope he hasn't taken anyone hostage."

"The crew hasn't turned up anything, either," said Jack. "Maids have gone through the rooms, the luggage areas, everywhere anyone could have hidden a stack of paintings, and we've got no leads."

"You worked with an artist to create a sketch, and they've circulated the picture of the man you saw in the gallery, but it's turned up nothing," Jack reported. "It's as if he disappeared into thin air."

"Maybe he jumped off the ship," Will suggested.

"Not with those priceless works of art," Jack said.

"I don't think we're ever going to find him," Kate despaired.

"We can't give up," Juliette said. "And we won't."

"I've been doing some Internet research on those paintings we saw," Kate said. "One of them was stolen from a Viennese Jewish family. It's been missing for seventy years, ever since the outbreak of World War II.

I have no idea how it could have ended up on this ship or how any of those paintings ended up here."

****

After lunch, Juliette stopped at the row of lounge chairs arranged under the deck.

"Kate and I will stay here out of the sun, order some drinks, and consult the universe."

"Consult the universe?" Will snarled. "What kind of hocus pocus is that?"

"It's best you don't ask, Will," Jack advised. "When the two of them get together, well, they're a powerful force you don't want to cross."

Jack turned to Kate. "Will and I will be here at the bar while you two commune with the cosmos."

"Jack, I'm a grown woman. I don't need you to babysit me."

Jack looked at Kate's stomach. "I think you do need a babysitter, and I told you I wasn't going to let you out of my sight."

Kate sighed.

"You told him." Juliette smiled.

"Yes, and he is becoming even more protective of me, if that's possible."

"He loves you. I think it's sweet."

"It's not as if we're in any real danger."

Juliette looked heavenward, where some ominous clouds were forming over the ship in an otherwise clear sky.

"That's not clear. I think we are in danger, until that murderer is apprehended. So let's get to work. And if Wade Randall or whatever his real name is turns out to be our murderer, he now has my cabin number, which I foolishly provided on that bidding form."

Kate shivered.

Kate and Juliette settled into their lounge chairs. A girl came over and took their drink order and then left them alone after she'd brought their drinks.

Juliette took Kate's hand.

"Now, I want you to concentrate. Clear out all extraneous thoughts. Focus on that night we were in the gallery. He must have been disguised, so focus on the man's eyes, his thoughts. See if we can locate him, for surely he's still aboard this ship."

Kate drained her mind of all thoughts of the baby, Jack, the business. She felt the temperature drop and tightened the terrycloth bathing suit cover-up around her shoulders. Juliette was controlling her mind now. She was in some kind of a trancelike state. Juliette still had hold of her hand.

"Do you see him?"

Kate nodded.

"Describe what you see."

"He's in shadows, but I know it's him, and he's watching me, watching us."

"Do you see the paintings?"

"No." Kate kept her eyes closed and concentrated. When she opened them, a ghostlike figure swept by. He was tall, dressed in deck shoes, jeans, a navy golf shirt, and a black parka, with the hood partially covering his bearded face. He glided by so quickly it was as if she'd imagined him.

"There." Kate pointed toward to the elevator, shouting to Jack and Will. "That's him."

Juliette opened her eyes. A large crow lighted on her deck chair. "I saw what you saw."

"Was he real?"

"It was definitely him."

Jack and Will ran toward the elevator, pressed the button, and rode it to an upper floor.

Then a long shadow fell across Kate's chair and a man towered over them, blocking the sun. Kate removed her sunglasses.

Juliette placed her arm protectively across Kate's stomach, and her breath caught in her throat. "It's you."

"Ilona." The name came out like a song on a breeze; then a chilly wind swept up and swirled around her. "I know it's you. Did you think you could hide from me? Did you think I wouldn't recognize you after all this time?" He paused and whispered seductively, "I've come to take you home."

Juliette tightened her hold on Kate.

"And you"—he turned to Kate—"stop looking for me. Don't get in my way, or you'll end up at the bottom of the ocean."

"Leave her alone," Juliette ordered, clutching the violet talisman around her neck.

"And, young lady, if you tell anyone you saw me, that will be the last thing you do. I'll find you and deal with you and that nosy detective husband of yours."

Kate shuddered and held on to Juliette's arm. She flung her other hand across her belly. Instinctively, Juliette placed her right hand on top of Kate's to protect the new life growing inside her.

Then, as fast as it had descended on them, the presence disappeared.

"What was that?" Kate asked.

"Ageless evil. Some kind of wicked incarnation of the man we saw in the gallery, maybe the man himself. He could have been projecting his image. One minute he was running across the deck in the opposite direction, and the next he was here at our side."

"Is that even possible?"

"You can exist and communicate on two levels and be in two different places at the same time. I've seen things. Things I can't forget. He is hypnotic. He is trying to feed on my power. I've never seen anything like it, not over here, anyway."

"What do you mean, 'not over here'? And why did he call you Ilona?"

Juliette sighed. "It's a long story. Maybe I'll tell you some day. But right now, we have to find Jack and Will and warn them. They're no match for this man. "He's very powerful. A true dark spirit."

"He looked like a vampire, like in those movies and TV shows."

"In the way he moves, yes. And his aversion to the sun."

"There aren't really vampires, are there, Juliette?"

Juliette stiffened. "I've learned not to rule anything out. I believe anything's possible. But this one is smooth and cunning. He wants what he wants, and I have a feeling he always gets what he wants. If those paintings are worth what you say they are, then he will do anything to protect them. We need to increase protection on the summit conferees. And you must never be out of my sight or Jack's. He claims he's after me, but the man sees you as an impediment, and he'll stop at nothing if he thinks you're in his way."

Jack and Will strode toward Kate and Juliette.

"It's like he dissolved before our eyes," Jack said as he reached them. "We were chasing him into the elevator, and suddenly he was gone. He was running, and then—it was as if he materialized in another dimension. He must be a magician."

"Don't underestimate him," Juliette said. "If he's a magician, then he's practicing black magic. He's more than a simple art thief. He's very dangerous."

Will covered Juliette with his windbreaker. "Juliette, you're shaking, and the sun is shining in the sky."

"Thank you," Juliette said, wrapping her arms around herself.

"We, um, had an encounter with our art thief," Kate explained.

"You saw him again?" Jack asked.

"Yes. You went after him, but suddenly he was right in front of us, blotting out the sun. He warned us to stop looking for him, or else…"

"He threatened you?" Jack paced the deck.

"And you," Juliette whispered, her voice shaking.

"He seemed to know Juliette," Kate said, "but I know that's not possible."

"Okay, we need to find this man soon. We're going to be docking in Bermuda, and he'll try to get off the ship. We don't have much time. I'm going to go see the captain. Kate, you're coming with me."

Jack helped Kate out of her lounge chair, kept hold of her hand, and they headed toward the elevators.

"He blotted out the sun?" Will asked, lowering himself onto the chair Kate had just vacated.

"Yes," Juliette replied. "He's much more dangerous than I thought."

"You make him sound like a monster."

"In a way, that's just what he is," Juliette said. "He's killed for his artwork, and he'll not hesitate to kill again."

Will stared at Juliette. All the color had gone from her face.

"What aren't you telling me?"

Juliette blew out a breath.

"I never wanted to talk about it again. It's been such a long time. I thought I-I'd forgotten. I tried to forget. I didn't want to tell my daughter."

Will pick up Juliette's hand and held it.

"You can tell me anything, Juliette. Does this man remind you of the Reverend Carter Coulter?"

Juliette shuddered. "Carter was evil, but not on this level. There is something truly malevolent about this man. I recognize his spirit. There was a man…"

Juliette bit her lip.

"A man… Go ahead," Will prompted.

"I told you I was from Hungary. I was born into a family of gypsies, Roma. But we're called many things. We had no permanent home; we moved from place to place. And then, one day, we settled on the land outside a grand castle. The estate was isolated, desolate, near the top of a hill—a mountain, really—in the hinterlands, near Transylvania. The count who ruled that land was evil. He permitted us to live on his property, but for a price. It was my mother who paid that price. She was the most beautiful woman in all the land.

"Every night, after dusk, she would go up to his castle made of stone, many stories high, and stay until dawn the next morning. She would come down from the castle, bruised and disheveled, her head hung low, but with a large basket full of fruits and candies and fresh honey from the count's drowsy bees, the finest bottle of red wine, fresh-baked breads and cakes of all kinds, and all manner of meats and cheeses. Food fit for a king. So we would have a feast, my mother and I.

" 'What happened to you?' I would ask her repeatedly. For it seemed that this man had feasted on my mother. She shook her head. But I could see that she was smeared with evil. We did not have a protector. I never knew my father, although my mother said he was a prince from a faraway land and that they had fallen in love. But when I was born, the prince's wife, who was barren, came to my mother intending to drive her off the land. She planned to steal her child and pass me off as her own. So my mother bundled me up and we left the land before my mother had a chance to say goodbye to her prince, her one true love."

"Sounds like a fairy tale," said Will. "A dark fairy tale."

"And now my mother seemed to be under another man's spell. 'That is our curse,' my mother said. 'We are irresistible to men.' We never saw the man during the day, and when he did appear at the edge of his property, he was draped in black from the brim of his top hat to his leather wingtips. He would put out a hand as if he was waving an invisible wand, and my mother sprang up as if in a trance and walked up the hill with him to his castle.

"Every day, it was the same. She would come back down alone, her lips swollen, bites across her breasts and on her neck, but with a basket full of sweets. And every morning, it was our ritual, I would bathe her and treat her wounds. And we would enjoy the feast. 'Does it hurt?' I would ask. 'No, my child. Not much,' she would reply.

"Months later, she removed the amethyst talisman on the long silver chain from around her neck and placed it around mine. It had been a gift from the prince, my father. She had never taken it off before. 'You have the gift of sight. You have powers I could never dream of. And remember, no one can take your powers away from you—unless you let them. Your road will be difficult and sometimes dangerous,' she cautioned, 'but one day you will find happiness and true love like I've known.' "

"How old were you then?" Will asked.

"I was fifteen, still a child, but I looked much older than my age. I was beginning to get second glances, leering looks, from boys and men who would come by to do business with the man in the castle. I could feel the count's eyes on me from a high window in the castle. My mother gathered up some belongings— clothes, food, and gold coins she had saved. 'Take this and run,' she said. 'Get as far away as you can from this wicked place. Go across the ocean. I love you.' She kissed me and held me tight. 'I have heard the women in the castle talk. Tomorrow he will come for me and make me his forever. You must not be here. He has taken an abnormal interest in you and wants to make you his own. That was the price I paid. I offered him my body if he would leave you alone, and soon I will no longer interest him. He is not satisfied with only me. I will not be coming back down to the camp after tonight, so please, I beg you, leave now.' "

Will was patient, waiting for Juliette to continue, but when she was quiet, he spoke. "What happened then?"

"The ladies gathered around to bathe and dress my

mother in the finest silk gown, a wedding gown, I think, and arranged her hair and placed a sparkling diamond tiara on her head, with jewels fit for a queen. They whispered that she was the chosen one. How lucky that the count had sent for her. She was beautiful, a sacrificial bride. She walked slowly but with no hesitation up to the castle, sometimes slipping, but with her head held high. That was the last time I saw my mother. I screamed her name, but she never look back. I think he had some kind of hold on her. 'Where's your power?' I cried out to her. But I knew she had given it to me."

Will covered Juliette's hand protectively with both of his. "That must have been frightening for a child your age to bear. How did you manage all alone? How did you come to be in Casa Spirito, in Florida, such a long way from your home?"

"That's just it. We never really had a permanent home. I rode out of the property with a man in a wagon who was on his way to Calais. From there I was to buy passage to England and then on to America. But when the man stole most of my gold coins, I was forced to work until I had enough money to pay for my passage. I could have sold my necklace, but it was my only connection to my mother, and I couldn't bear to part with it. Once I got to America, I was alone and terribly lonely, drifting from city to city, until I met Carter and I thought I was finally home. I thought he was the man my mother spoke of. My true love."

"The Reverend Carter Coulter, the man who fathered Kate? The man you killed?"

Juliette nodded and retold the story.

"In the beginning, Carter Coulter was like a savior.

He took me in, set me up in my own shop. It was the first time in a long time I'd had any kind of stability. I owed him everything. I told him I would repay his kindness, but he didn't want my money. He said he recognized my talent. He was also very powerful. I…I f-fell in love with him—or I fell under his spell. And by the time I realized he was just using me, I was pregnant, with no place to go, and then when she was born he stole my daughter from me."

"He was twice your age, married, and he took advantage of you." Will removed one of his hands from Juliette's and flexed his fist. "And many other women, from what I've read. The bastard got what he deserved. Carter Coulter was evil, just as the count of that castle was evil and the man in the gallery, the man on this ship, is evil."

Juliette started to shake, and Will held her close.

"You're not alone anymore, and you're not that same young, naïve girl." Will placed a kiss on Juliette's forehead. "You have Kate and Jack, and now you have me. And you are a strong woman, Juliette. I'm glad you feel like you can confide in me, that you can trust me."

Juliette looked at Will hopefully, and the wall she'd erected between them began to crumble.

"I've been fooled by love before," Juliette said. *Maybe this time will be different.*

Chapter Fourteen

The resemblance was uncanny. Ilona was the picture of her mother, Marika. A picture Gedeon had stared at and salivated over for the past two decades. A picture of the woman he had yearned for ever since Marika's beautiful soul had deserted him, fled this world and left him miserable and alone in his castle. The castle, massive and rich, was situated on a large, placid lake. There were a hundred castles and ruins in Hungary. His was one of the most magnificent. Built on a rocky hill near the eastern border of Transylvania, the residence was difficult to get to but offered a panoramic view of the region. Inside, the Gothic-Renaissance structure boasted a tower, wine cellars, and an underground prison.

In his opinion, the painting he had commissioned of her mother was more mystifying than the Mona Lisa, more compelling than the *Girl with a Pearl Earring*. Once you saw it, you couldn't look away. It was entrancing. She was entrancing. The painting didn't do her justice. And this girl must be her daughter. Had to be. So strange to see Ilona roaming this far from home.

Marika. Dark and beautiful, just like this woman below him on the Lido deck. Marika's daughter. All grown up. And who was the beauty that she so resembled, asleep in the next lounge chair?

His eyes bored into Ilona's soul, observing her,

studying her face from his dark hiding place behind a post on the deck above. A face he thought he'd never see again. Gedeon's pulse raced. Although he was out of the sun, sweat glistened on his brow. He throbbed under his pants.

Marika's daughter had run away. Vanished in the night. He had been furious. He'd wanted her to join in the wedding festivities. He had special plans for her. He had punished Marika mercilessly to find out where she had gone, but Marika wouldn't talk.

Then he had healed her and brought in a famous Hungarian artist to paint her—a full portrait—that immortalized her but barely captured her magic—her beauty, fire, and power. He would sit for hours pining away before the picture, while the flesh-and-blood subject rotted away in chains in his castle's dank prison. Every time he'd summoned her, she'd refused him. When she was completely submissive, starving, with no fight left, he would free her, have her brought to his bed, and when he was done with her, have her returned to the dungeon in chains. Until one day, when his slap to awaken her brought no response. She had taken her last traitorous breath. His beloved Marika—his butterfly—was dead. Gone from him forever—until now.

The screams that echoed off the castle walls that night after Marika died bled through the limestone. How dare she escape from him? He had left her body there to rot, in the billowing wedding gown, until she was nothing but bones. Where was her power and glory now?

So it became more important than ever to find her daughter, Ilona, who would be offered up to him in her place, to Gedeon, whose name meant Warrior, Devastater. He had hungered for her that night Marika's spirit left this earth. He couldn't wait to taste Ilona and have her in his bed. He had sent out messengers all over Europe to find her. The room at the castle had been carefully prepared. Candles, wine, flowers, everything to please his new bride-to-be. He had watched her from his window for months while he was entertaining Marika. She was young and ripe, only fifteen, but already so beautiful and womanly. And he would be the first to deflower her.

When he'd placed Marika in the dungeon he had sent for Ilona, and when his guards reported that Ilona had disappeared, escaped with a man in a wagon in the middle of the night like a thief, he had raged against fate and destroyed the bedroom. Ripped the gold-threaded white sheets to tatters, smashed the heavy silver candlesticks to the floor, swept the sweetmeats and other delicacies across the table with a broad sweep of his hands. Broke against the wall the bottle of the best sparkling wine, a sweet aphrodisiac he'd ordered to drug her and put her in the mood, and backhanded the messenger.

"There will be other girls," his chief advisor had assured him. "Even more desirable. She was only a gypsy, like her mother, a plaything to be used, nothing of consequence, not worthy of a man of your position."

Gedeon rose up to his full height and bellowed, "I will not be denied. She was promised to me. She was mine. I want her back. I want no other man to have her."

"Too bad you can't ask your whore where her daughter went. I could bring her to you, but she's a little ripe."

Gedeon slapped the arrogant man across his face like an angry bear.

"Don't touch Marika. She was mine to pleasure and to punish as I wished."

And, for his insolence, Gedeon gutted him where he stood and took great pleasure in watching him bleed out.

Drunk, angry, and eager for vengeance, Gedeon roamed the hills that night, taking by force what he felt should have been provided as his due. Mothers in the town learned to lock up their daughters for their own protection when Gedeon was on his rampage.

Gedeon suffered a hereditary condition. He was allergic to sunlight. He couldn't travel during the day. So as he roamed, restless, through the cobblestone streets of the town in darkness, the locals began to fear the dreaded night prowler.

When he returned, inebriated, he would make his way cautiously down to the castle dungeon where the paintings were stored. One evening, in an amorous mood, he selected a large canvas, a particularly sensual depiction of a mythological scene by Titian, commissioned by some corrupt, womanizing cardinal or another back in the 1500s. It was one of the painter's erotic mythologies of a beautiful maiden reclining in the nude, with the face of the cardinal's mistress, about to receive one of the gods. Piety was overrated in the sixteenth century.

Enthralled, he propped it up against a stack of similar paintings. Spent from carousing all night, he collapsed onto a huge chair, looked over at Marika's body, still clothed in her bridal gown, hanging in chains, and fell into a slumberous trance of ecstasy. He imagined the reclining nude was Marika's body and the striking face of the courtesan was Marika's face. And that he could still taste and touch her beautiful curves and crevasses. He had confined her. She had resisted. And, in the end, Gedeon had triumphed. Now she was his for all eternity.

But what good does it do to survive multiple lifetimes with no one by your side? All his riches couldn't compensate for the devastating tsunami of loneliness. Loneliness that could only be eased with Marika, his soulmate. He and Marika were destined to be together. And now that she was gone, Ilona must be his consolation. But even with all his wealth and power he couldn't find Ilona. Until now.

Gedeon had rubbed his beard thoughtfully and slowly licked his lips. The painting was splendid—extraordinary, really. Female nudity and erotic subject matter were Titian's specialties, particular themes of his. In the Michelangelos, the nudes were draped with white sheets for propriety's sake. He much preferred the Titians that had been commissioned by monarchs and hidden in churches or personal collections across Europe but were now his. He was more powerful than any pope or king. Their royal bones were buried in vaults somewhere, while Gedeon was still flourishing.

Selling the paintings in his extensive collection, one canvas at time, provided Gedeon with a steady income. He was already rich when German forces occupied Hungary during World War II and appropriated his castle. When the last of the Fascist Arrow Cross Party vacated the country in 1945, they left in haste, with the vengeful Russians hot on their trail, leaving thousands of framed and unframed artworks, paintings and tapestries stolen from the homes of fleeing or captured Jews, a priceless collection, a treasure trove of masterpieces of incalculable worth that they had crated and stored in the castle's cellar. His castle was one of many Nazi storage depots scattered throughout Europe.

Masterpieces by Monet, van Gogh, Cézanne, Picasso, Matisse, Renoir, and Chagall, and a collection of forbidden or so-called degenerate art by controversial modern artists, even Impressionists and Old Masters. Treasures thought to be lost forever. Treasures that remained out of sight for decades. Treasures that had increased in value.

For years, the paintings stayed hidden, until the world had forgotten them. Gedeon had hired trusted intermediaries, releasing some works periodically to private collectors, public museums, gallery owners, and dealers, timed to get the maximum profit. The looted Nazi art served as an unlimited source of his wealth for decades, and the fortune offered protection from the Soviets or whatever current force was in power. And he had kept meticulous records in his diary regarding where the paintings were sold, to whom, and for what amount. He also kept the Nazi records of where the paintings and other works of art had come from. It never hurt to have insurance.

Sometimes Gedeon himself traveled the continent and abroad, selling the paintings to the highest bidder, falsifying provenances, enriching his coffers. In all that time, he had never found another woman he could love. Never found another woman like Marika. Never stopped wanting Ilona to take her place.

But now, here she was. Fate had delivered Ilona to him. He could have her, and he would have her. Soon. He and Ilona were kindred spirits. Soulmates. They had a history. Of course, she would have to be punished for running away. But the naughty child had grown to be a desirable woman, very much like her mother in form and feature.

He wouldn't make the same mistake he'd made with Marika. Leaving her in chains to rot. He would bring Ilona back to the castle. In chains, yes, at first, to break her spirit. But if she behaved, and submitted to him, he would forgive her, and then they could live together forever. But first, there was the matter of the paintings. He would deliver them to the buyer in Bermuda. He would have to delay his plans to deliver the rest of the artwork to the collectors in the States. First, he would deal with Ilona. He was eager to bring her back to the castle, where she belonged. Where *they* belonged. It was her home.

Chapter Fifteen

Juliette and Kate sat on chairs out on the balcony of Kate's suite, watching the waves created by the ship's wake. Juliette had hardly slept last night. Dark restless thoughts of the past had invaded her mind. No wonder she was exhausted.

Kate closed the bestseller she was reading, marked her place, and balanced the book on her lap.

"The view is amazing, but I feel like a prisoner," lamented Kate. "We're trapped on this ship, and Jack and Will won't let us out of their sight."

"How do you think I feel, being trapped in my cabin with the oversexed police chief? He won't stop touching me. I know this togetherness is for our own protection, but any minute now I'm going to jump out of my skin."

"I thought he might grow on you, being in such close quarters."

"Too close. Of course they gave us a king-sized bed, since we're on our 'honeymoon.' That is more than awkward. And he is plying me with bottles of wine in our cabin, compliments of the captain. It's not that I don't find him attractive. I find him too attractive. But he tries to take liberties every chance he gets."

"Jack told me he finds you irresistible. That it was a curse. What did he mean by that?"

"Oh, nothing. Just men talking."

"They think we're helpless," objected Kate, who held on to her hat to keep it from blowing away in the breeze.

"We're far from it," Juliette stated. "In fact, if we wanted to, we could easily get away from them."

"What do you have in mind, jumping overboard?"

"Nothing that drastic. A simple slipaway spell. We'd be gone and they'd never even realize it."

"Can you really do that?"

"Yes, and so can you."

"It won't hurt them, will it? I'm kind of attached to my husband."

"I wish I weren't attached to mine, but no, it'll knock them out for a while, but they won't remember a thing."

Juliette reached into her beach bag and brought out a small pouch. From it she took a handful of tiny square crystals resembling sugar cubes. She placed them on top of Kate's book in a circular pattern and recited a chant, which she asked Kate to repeat. Gathering up the crystals, she opened the glass door into the cabin, walked to the coffeepot, and chirped sweetly, "Would you gentlemen like some coffee?"

Jack and Will, seated in chairs across from the bed, turned to her eagerly.

"I'd love some, Juliette," Jack said.

"Me too, angel face."

Juliette cringed.

"Coming right up." Juliette prepared two cups of coffee and slipped a pinch of the crystals into each man's cup. She brought the cups and saucers over to where Will and Jack were seated.

"Fair warning," she said. "It's pretty strong."

"Just like I like it, sugar." Will swatted her behind.

Juliette smiled sweetly. "Exactly."

Kate followed Juliette into the cabin.

Jack raised his coffee cup and drank it. Will did the same.

"Delicious," Jack said. "Juliette, you make the best coffee. We'll have to find out the brand and get it at home."

"Thank you, Jack. I think everything just tastes better on the open ocean. The sea increases your appetite."

Will winked at her. Then his jaw went slack and the empty cup slipped out of his hands and into Juliette's waiting ones.

Jack stared at Kate through vacant eyes. He held the cup, but he was barely conscious.

Juliette removed Jack's cup and placed the china on the table by the sink.

Jack's head lolled listlessly and came to rest on the back of the chair. Will was slumped over.

"Juliette, are you sure they're all right?"

"They're in la-la land, and when they wake up, we'll be back. For them, no time will have passed at all. Let's get out while we have a chance."

"How long do we have?"

"Oh, several hours, at least," Juliette said. "Let's make the most of it."

Juliette and Kate picked up their handbags and walked out of the room like the two co-conspirators they were. They walked down the hall and got on the elevator.

"Where to?" Kate asked.

Juliette pushed the button for the fifth floor. "Back

to the scene of the crime."

When they arrived at the gallery, yellow crime scene tape still crisscrossed the opening, but Juliette managed to get around it and held the tape up for her daughter.

"Didn't you say Jack received a report that all of the paintings we saw were stolen?"

"Yes, I was right. None of the heists was recent, though, so our thief and probable murderer sat on them for a long time. And he circulated the picture I drew of Wade Randall and didn't get a hit. We thought maybe the killer was an established art dealer, but that turned out to be a dead end."

The women returned to the spot where they had first met "Wade Randall."

"I still can't understand how he got these paintings on board and how he thinks he's going to offload them. The whole crew is looking for him."

"Perhaps he had some help," Juliette suggested. "Maybe the gallery manager, Pierre Dumas, is cooperating with our thief. I didn't like the look of him."

"That makes perfect sense," Kate reasoned. "Or it could be one of the crew. Wade could have bribed someone to help him. The captain is checking the crew and passenger manifests. Pierre Dumas claims there were no paintings hidden behind the paintings in the frames, but I think we need to recheck them ourselves, right now."

"I wouldn't have any idea how to do that," Juliette said.

"I do. In the gallery where I used to work, we were called on to do everything from framing to sales."

Kate began the tedious process of checking, painting by painting, to see if anyone had tampered with the frames. "I have a feeling we're overlooking the obvious. That the answer is right in front of us."

"Aren't we docking in Bermuda tomorrow?" Juliette wondered.

"Yes, and you know the killer will be disembarking, too. He won't want to stay on the ship. We're on the island for two nights. If he does decide to stay on the ship after it leaves Bermuda, then he'll offload the paintings on the island and have them mailed somewhere. Jack has alerted the police in Bermuda. I don't see how this man can get away."

"He'll only become more dangerous and enraged if he's cornered, like a wild animal that's trapped," Juliette predicted. "We really shouldn't be here alone. No one knows we're here, and he could return at any moment."

"I'm not finished checking these canvases," Kate said, working furiously, moving from painting to painting. "So far, I don't see anything out of the ordinary."

"I doubt he left something so valuable here," Juliette said. "Not at a crime scene. But he may be planning to come back during the auction."

"That would be very risky."

"I have known many evil men, and to them, risk is thrilling, part of the game."

Juliette checked her watch. "It's been several hours. We'd better be getting back to the cabin. Jack and Will may be waking up soon."

The women left the gallery and took the elevator back up to Kate's cabin. When they arrived, Jack and

Will were still sleeping off the effects of the slipaway spell.

Kate nudged Jack. "Jack, get up."

Juliette lifted Will's head. "Okay, cowboy, time to get up."

Will stirred and came awake. "Juliette?"

"Kate and I are hungry. How about taking us down to the dining room for dinner?"

Jack got up from his chair.

"I'm starving. Let's go. I must be more tired than I thought. I think I fell asleep."

"Me too," said Will. "What have you girls been up to? Working on your tans on the balcony?"

Kate and Juliette looked at each other. Both women were dark-skinned, both had been labeled mysterious-looking, and neither tanned easily.

"That's exactly what we've been doing," Juliette said.

Chapter Sixteen

The two couples arrived at the dining room and were seated by the window at a table for four. Most of the passengers had already eaten, and the dining room was almost empty.

"What a lovely view," said Juliette, looking at all the sparkly lights out the picture window as she opened her menu. The server poured each of them a glass of water and asked if they'd like anything else to drink. Will and Jack ordered beers, and the women decided on a sweet white wine—a Moscato d'Asti.

"What looks good?" Jack asked.

"Everything," said Kate. "I think I'll start with a bowl of the Bermuda fish chowder, since we're going to be in port tomorrow. It will get me in the mood. Then I'll have the Cornish game hen."

Juliette ordered the roast chicken. Will and Jack each ordered a twelve-ounce bone-in ribeye.

"So, Jack, what's next on our agenda?" Will asked, closing his menu.

"After dinner, we'll stop by and check on the conference. They're having an unscheduled night meeting. But the captain has assured me that other than the usual verbal disagreements, everything is quiet on the banking front. We're docking at the Heritage Wharf cruise ship terminal at the Royal Naval Dockyard in Bermuda first thing in the morning, and Kate and

Juliette, you'll need to be standing at the pier during disembarkation to make sure our thief doesn't slip by. You said the man we're looking for is tall and has a beard, but he may have shaved, and he may be wearing a disguise. After everyone has left the ship, we're free to explore, and while we're out, we're to keep our eyes open. The crew will do another thorough search of the cabins."

"Juliette tells me you're going to be our tour guides." Will lifted an eyebrow at Jack.

"Kate and I spent our honeymoon there, although we hardly left the room, so we're looking forward to this second chance to see the island."

Will inched his chair closer to Juliette while he questioned Jack. "How will we get around in Bermuda?"

"Well, there are buses, ferries, and taxis. But I thought it would be fun to rent motor scooters," said Jack. "Tourists aren't allowed to drive cars. Will, have you ever driven a cycle or a moped?"

"I used to be a traffic cop, so, yes. And I ride all the time at home."

"Great, then it's me and Kate and you and Juliette, on two-seaters."

Will squeezed Juliette's hand. "Have you ever been on a scooter before, sweetheart?"

"No," she said, her eyes widening at Will's new term of endearment. The reverend had never called her sweetheart. It felt good. She felt—loved.

"Nothing to be afraid of. Just hold on tight to me, and when I turn, you lean into the turn. Of course, you'll be wearing a helmet."

"Just be careful on the cycle," Kate warned. "In

Bermuda, remember, they drive on the left side of the road, the wrong side. And the roundabouts are killers. Everyone rents motor scooters, and they don't always know how to drive them. Invariably, they spill their mopeds and end up in the hospital with road rash."

"The food in Bermuda is amazing," Jack said, digging into his steak. "And I already have reservations at our favorite restaurant for tomorrow night, the Waterlot Inn at the Fairmont Hotel in Southampton. You can try Bermuda fish chowder, and fresh lobster if it's in season. But the restaurant specializes in steaks and chops."

"Then when we're in Hamilton, shopping, we thought we'd have lunch at the Lobster Pot," Kate said. "They have these sinfully delicious hot apple fritters smothered in whipped cream, great for dessert. I can almost taste them now."

"It all sounds lovely," said Juliette, wondering how she was going to resist Will when she was clinging to him for dear life on the back of a motor scooter. Will and whipped cream. She didn't even want to go there, but her traitorous mind had other ideas.

"And, of course, we'll have full afternoon tea at the Fairmont Hamilton Princess in town," Kate said. "I can't believe we're coming back to Bermuda so soon."

"It's our favorite place," said Jack, who glanced at Kate's belly and then into her eyes. "We made some beautiful memories."

Kate blushed.

"And don't forget the soft pink sandy beaches," Jack said. "And Will, Bermuda is a golfer's paradise."

"It doesn't sound like we'll have enough time to do everything you want to do."

"Well, we'll do as much as we can."

"Or nothing," said Kate. "That's the great thing about Bermuda. That, and the shopping."

"What kind of shopping?" Juliette asked.

"Well, the list is endless. There are authentic Bermuda cedar wood gifts, soaps made with island fragrances, jewelry—especially the Bermuda longtails —and the moon gates, gold coins, sailboats, fine china, and crystal imported from Europe. Not to mention the quality linens and local gourmet products such as rum and sherry pepper sauce, and Gosling's Black Seal® Rum, used to make the Dark'n'Stormy and Rum Swizzle cocktails. Front Street is a hub for shopping in big stores like A.S. Cooper & Sons Limited or in small boutiques."

"What's a moon gate?" Juliette asked.

"Moon gates are a traditional architectural element in Bermuda. They're a symbol of the island, and you can find them all over. They're stone arches typically found at garden entrances, usually free-standing or attached to a low wall. You can buy little replicas in the shops, just like you can buy Eiffel Tower replicas in Paris. They say that couples who kiss under a moon gate or make a wish as they step through the moon gate hand in hand are granted happiness and good fortune during their marriage and will have a long and happy life together."

"We'll have to find a moon gate, Juliette, and walk through it to guarantee us a happy ending," said Will.

"Our marriage will be ending as soon as we debark," said Juliette. "I don't think even a moon gate will make a difference, in our case." And the thought of that made her sad.

Chapter Seventeen

The ship's photographer was snapping pictures of every passenger who left the ship, whether they wanted to pose or not. Just a second layer of security. Standing next to the photographer, Kate and Juliette tried to blend into the background.

"My eyes are starting to bug out," Juliette complained.

The last single man walked off the ship, slathered in sunscreen, wearing over-sized sunglasses and sporting a sagging paunch, barely contained by a flowered button-down shirt, which fit loosely over khaki shorts. He walked up to Juliette and put his arm around her.

"Pose with me, pretty lady?"

Juliette sighed. To protect her cover, she had no choice. This was the umpteenth man to proposition her.

Juliette frowned, and the tourist, who looked like he belonged in Disneyland or a botanical garden, smiled like he had just won the lottery.

The photographer went to work.

"Do you know you look like a gypsy?" Flowered Shirt Guy said.

"I get that a lot," Juliette said, the smile frozen like bad botox on her face.

The photographer signaled that she had the shot she needed. "You can find your picture in the lounge outside the dining room tonight when you reboard the ship."

"Why don't you read my fortune, Gypsy Lady?" said the man, pulling at Juliette's hand and placing his greasy one in her palm.

Hanging on to his composure by a thread, Will stood like a sphinx in front of Flowered Shirt Guy but finally moved into action. "Move along now, buddy, and get your hands off my wife."

The passenger slipped away after measuring Will's bulk and menacing looks.

"Thanks for rescuing me."

"I seem to be doing that a lot. Do men always hit on you?"

"Unfortunately, yes."

"Oh, that's right, you're irresistible to men."

"It's a curse."

Jack bounded over to where Kate and Juliette were standing.

"They've cut us loose. That's the last of the passengers. Let's explore Bermuda. I've got our cycles all lined up, over there."

Jack took Kate's hand and Will grabbed Juliette's.

"You look like you could use a massage, honey." Will placed his hands at the back of Juliette's neck and started kneading.

Juliette rounded on him. "And you look like the guy who wants to give me one. All I want is to get on that motor scooter and fly. Work out some of those kinks."

At the motorcycle livery, Will pulled up a red two-seater in front of the waiting Juliette.

"I've got your ride, ma'am," said Will. He fastened

her helmet strap under Juliette's chin before he put on his own helmet. "Just hop on and hold on tight."

Jack and Kate were already on their motor scooter ahead of them. Will had arranged to follow Jack into Hamilton.

When the scooter engine revved up, Juliette startled and tightened her arms around Will's stomach. She hoped he wasn't some grandstander. She'd never been on a motorbike before. This trip was full of firsts. First cruise, first marriage, first fake marriage…

Will looked back. "Now, remember, when I lean right, you lean right. When I lean left, you lean left. Don't fight me." He seemed to be talking about more than just riding the cycle. Juliette held on as Will pulled the scooter out into traffic. She locked her fingers together. It was like riding a roller coaster. She wanted to scream. She wanted to fly. She never wanted to get off. And then she couldn't stop smiling.

Will's body felt solid against her chest. His abs were as strong as steel. Not an ounce of fat on his body. He probably worked out. He was in good shape for a small-town sheriff. For any man. After a few rough starts, she followed his lead and leaned in the direction he was taking the scooter. The warm wind blew against her face. She closed her eyes and then ventured a look at the beautiful houses whizzing by. Spots of aqua, yellow, green, white—an architectural rainbow flashed in front of her. The white roofs, the limestone walls, the gardens. Oh, the gardens! She took in the blue sky and the turquoise water and pressed her face into Will's back, breathing in his scent. Will Bradley was getting harder and harder to resist and easier and easier to be around.

Chapter Eighteen

Juliette shuddered. Her thoughts drifted back to the last time she had seen Marika in Hungary. The shadow of the stone castle over them, saying goodbye to her mother, saying goodbye to the light, fearing the cold, long journey ahead. She hadn't thought about the giant, evil, bearded man in all these years. He should be ancient by now, so this man on the ship must be his grandson. Or had she imagined the resemblance? Was it just a nightmare? Or a premonition?

Will shook her awake. "Juliette, you were having a bad dream. It's okay. You're okay." Will's strong arms wound around her. She was cold in her flimsy nightgown, but Will's arms were like a raging fire, warm and welcoming.

Her nightgown slipped, revealing a tanned breast and a pink nipple. She started to cover up and caught Will staring hungrily at her. For the first time she let him look. Wanted him to look. Her nipples hardened. Something was happening. Will stirred emotions she hadn't felt in a long time. Too long. He placed a chaste kiss on her forehead, but his eyes revealed that his thoughts were anything but chaste. Nor were hers.

Next his lips were on hers, soft and gentle, and his tongue teased her mouth open.

"Will," she sighed, responding. His drugging kisses carried her away. He touched her breast and pressed his body to hers, and she felt him through the sheer gown. She was still sore from riding the motorcycle all day, but it had been exhilarating. She'd loved the feel of her arms around Will and the sun warming her face and the wind in her hair. Smiling at the memory, she relaxed and went limp.

Leaving her lips, Will moved his mouth down her neck with fluttering kisses, took a breast in his hand and licked her nipple, and then took it into his mouth. His hand slid gently down her legs and up again until it reached her panties. She startled. His fingertips touched the outside of her panty line, then rubbed her panties until his hand crept inside and stroked her until she moaned. In response, Juliette moved against him. She was still sore at the core of her, but at his featherlight touch a gushy wetness flooded her panties, and she thrashed and bucked against his hand, wanting to scream out in satisfaction. When Will sensed she couldn't stand it anymore, he pulled down his briefs, found her, and thrust inside again and again. He collapsed on her and their measured breaths rose and fell in sync. They stayed that way, frozen in their respective positions, afraid to move.

What had just happened?

Will was the first to speak.

"You were pretty noisy," Will teased, raising his head with some effort.

"It's been a long time," Juliette joked.

"You don't see me complaining. I've been wanting to make love to you from the moment I met you. And you fought me every step of the way. What changed?"

"You changed. I trust you. And, you make me laugh. I want to laugh again."

Will held her tightly. "You've had a rough life, sweetheart. I know that, and that evil man, the reverend character…"

"Had me under his spell. I thought I was in love, but it wasn't love. It was all about power and control. I was too young and naïve to know the difference. And I needed him—needed someone—at the time."

Juliette nestled into Will to ward off all thoughts of another evil presence. A presence she was convinced was still on this ship.

She had a feeling he would make his move tomorrow in Bermuda. It was their last day on the island, and after that, he would follow through on his threats. He knew her as Ilona. No one else knew that name but the man in the castle, or perhaps the man's grandson. She was anxious to know what had happened to her mother. Was she still alive? Was she happy? Was she still in Hungary? Did she know where her daughter was? Did she miss her?

Juliette wondered if she should tell Will and Jack. They would think she was crazy if she told them an evil vampire-like presence had invaded her thoughts and stowed away on the ship. No, this was her battle to fight. She didn't want to involve her daughter. Kate must be protected at all costs. Kate and her unborn child.

"Must have been some dream, huh?" Will prodded. "Want to tell me about it?"

Juliette shook her head and dismissed Will's concerns, smoothing her hand across his naked chest. "I can barely remember it. It was nothing. Everything seems scarier in the darkness."

"Well, I'm here with you now, Juliette, my little

gypsy, so no more bad dreams, no more bad days, only sunny days ahead," Will assured. "Waking up here in bed with you, really with you, is a dream come true for me."

The light crept through the sheer curtains. But Juliette didn't want the night to end. She didn't want this time with Will to end. It brought to mind the infamous lines her namesake recited in Shakespeare's *Romeo and Juliet*. "It was the nightingale, and not the lark…believe me, love, it was the nightingale."

"Will, I don't know what to say."

"Don't *say* anything." Will stretched like a satisfied Cheshire cat and flashed a mischievous grin. He proceeded to move his naked body against Juliette's, placing fluttering kisses on the tip of her nose, her eyelids, her forehead, her cheeks, and her lips.

Responding to his amorous advances, Juliette lifted her arms over her head to give him better access to her breasts and lower body parts, which inflamed Will even more.

"Juliette, my love," he whispered. "I can't get enough of you." His mouth found her nipples, and he teased her with his tongue while his fingers explored her until she was writhing beneath him.

"I want, I want—" she panted.

"Tell me what you want, Juliette. I want to satisfy you."

Juliette twisted her body as an orgasm threatened to rip through her body with the power of an earthquake.

"I want you inside of me, Will, now," she cried out ecstatically, her arms pinned above her head as he moved his mouth back to hers. As he drove into her again and again, she moved against him, taking him deeper and deeper inside.

Will collapsed on top of her, forcing an "I love you," to whoosh out of her.

Winded, Will looked into Juliette's violet eyes. "Did I hear the "L" word?"

Juliette smiled. "Did *I*?"

"I don't think there's anything wrong with our hearing," he said. "I'm in love with you, Juliette Spencer." He paused, waiting for a response. "And this is the part where you say…"

Juliette reached up and kissed Will on the lips. "I think I might be in love with you, Will Bradley."

"You think? You think? You don't know?" Will feigned distress.

"I would be up to a repeat performance, just to verify my feelings."

"You've worn this old body out, Juliette, for the moment. I love you, and I'll shout it out to everyone in Bermuda. I'll never get tired of saying it."

"And I'll never get tired of hearing it."

Will took Juliette in his arms and gave her a possessive squeeze with a grip as tight as a boa constrictor's.

When Juliette recovered her breath, she sprang from the bed and opened the French doors to the balcony. Fishing boats and pleasure craft dotted the crowded harbor. The unique architecture of the island took center stage: pastel cottages—sky blue, yellow, sea green, and lilac, with white-limestone roofs and colorful doors and shutters—nestled in the cliffs and dramatic rock formations. The island was blessed with pristine pink sand beaches and turquoise water. And the flowers—calla lilies, iris, oleander, hibiscus, bougainvillea, and bermudiana—added to the island's fragrant scent. There were beautiful beach vistas everywhere you looked. There was a new day to explore, and she was anxious to get started.

"Let's get dressed and go down for breakfast. I can't wait to see the rest of the island. We had so much fun yesterday, exploring, going to all the beaches. You're beet red, Will Bradley. You need to wear sunscreen today. And a hat. The sun here is stronger than you think."

"You just look more tanned and more beautiful, Juliette. The sun agrees with you."

"You think I'm beautiful?"

"Best-looking woman on the ship, in my opinion," said Will. "And I'm the luckiest man, to be married to you."

Juliette laughed.

Will joined Juliette on their balcony and folded her in his arms protectively. It had been a long time since she had felt so coveted or heard such praise. Certainly not from the reverend, who had tried to diminish her at every turn. And when Will talked of their marriage, he sounded sincere. Could his feelings be real? What would that be like? To be in a normal relationship. And for the first time she entertained thoughts of a real love and a real partnership.

"This might be the prettiest view I've ever seen," Will said, looking at her meaningfully. "What's on the schedule today?"

"Well, Kate and Jack want to take us to dinner tonight at a place called the Waterlot Inn at the Fairmont Southampton. And I know Jack wants to check out some of the local galleries, to see if anyone suspicious has come in inquiring about selling any paintings. Although Kate says the man would not be out in the open dealing with a gallery. He would have other, more nefarious, contacts. The thief may already have left the ship and has probably already chartered a boat, or found another way off the island. But I'm afraid he's not done with us."

"He doesn't want to hang around, believe me. He wants to get as far away from this ship as possible. You heard what the captain said. We don't need to follow him. We'll just go about enjoying ourselves as if we're regular tourists. He'll be following us. He knows you and Kate can identify him, so wherever we go, he won't be far behind. Jack and I will be there to protect you, but we're going to have to be careful. You're his unfinished business, and after he takes care of loose ends, he's free to disappear."

The thief and murderer has a new mission, Juliette thought. A mission that has nothing to do with stolen art.

Chapter Nineteen

Kate, Juliette, Jack, and Will were dining alfresco on the Lido deck.

"This breakfast is just delicious," said Juliette, stabbing a fresh piece of pineapple with her fork and popping it into her mouth. "And I don't just mean the food. This view is fabulous, and it's just as amazing in the morning as it is at night, with all the lights twinkling against the cliffs. It's paradise."

"Mark Twain said it best when he wrote, 'You can go to heaven if you want; I'd rather stay in Bermuda,' " quoted Kate, taking Jack's hand. "I wish everyone could experience Bermuda. It has so much to offer. I hope we can come back every year."

"This has been the best vacation, or rather working vacation, in my life. Wife, don't you agree?" Will asked.

Juliette laughed and let Will bring her hand to his lips to kiss. Will twisted his fingers around Juliette's dark ringlets, and she didn't object. In fact, she inclined her head toward him, and he kissed her neck.

Kate raised her eyebrows, gave Jack a glance filled with suspicion, and then looked back at Juliette.

She senses there is something different between us, Juliette thought. And there is. I'm truly happy, for the first time in a long time, and it shows. Will Bradley got to me. He finally wore me down, and now I'm vulnerable to him. I just hope he doesn't hurt me like I've been hurt before.

"Well," said Jack. "Let's be the first people off the ship. I want to run in to some of the local galleries right here at the Royal Naval Dockyard, in the Clocktower Shopping Mall, and then we'll check out some galleries at the Bermuda craft market and the Bermuda Arts Centre at the Dockyard. After that, we'll go into Hamilton and check out some of the other local galleries. I'm not very optimistic. I don't think the thief can just drop by any art gallery and pawn his wares. I think he's had this caper planned for quite some time. He is probably meeting with some wealthy islander who can't wait to get his hands on these masterpieces, to admire them in his own home and then put them into a vault somewhere, locked away where no one can enjoy them."

"In that case, honey, what can we do about it?" Kate asked.

"Unfortunately, nothing," Jack said, waiting for Kate to get up before he stood. "Not if we can't locate those paintings or that Wade Randall character."

Jack led the way while the four flashed their ID cards into the scanner and walked off the ship into the Dockyard. Jack and Kate took half of the galleries and Will and Juliette scoped out the other half. No one admitted to seeing a man who had tried to sell them any artwork. They certainly would have recognized the pieces and alerted authorities.

"Well, if you see anyone fitting this description," Jack said, showing the picture the sketch artist had done from Kate and Juliette's memory, "be sure to call my cell phone." He left his business card.

"Let's take a taxi into town," Jack suggested, and they all piled in and asked to be driven to Hamilton.

"Wow, I love this place," said Juliette. "Everything is so colorful. There's so much to do here, so many shops, I don't know where to go first."

"Well, we have the whole day, so we have plenty of time to enjoy ourselves. Let's take a quick peek into that Irish linen shop, and then I'd like to take home some English bone china. And there's a map shop down the street that has wonderful original antique botanical prints, with hand coloring, that are over a hundred years old. And Juliette, I'd like to buy you a gold moon gate charm on a chain. I think you'd love that."

"It all sounds so wonderful," said Juliette. "Lead the way, and I'll follow."

"We'll be right behind you," said Will.

The danger they'd felt the previous day seemed to have faded. The sunshine boded well for a rosy future. The colors were light and lovely. But things could change in an instant, Juliette knew. They had changed for her before, in a flash.

Once, she had been a happy child with a lovely mother, cherished and cared for on her father's estate. The best clothes, the best horses, the best of everything. She was treated like a princess. But then her father had taken a bride in an arranged marriage, and she and her mother were turned away with only the clothes on their backs and the prince's priceless amethyst amulet around her mother's neck.

They didn't have roots, but they had each other. They traveled whenever the mood hit them. They sang. They rejoiced in life, until they got to Hungary. Visions of the castle and the evil man who lived there still haunted her nightmares. And this man she'd seen on the ship resembled the count of that castle—but that, of course, was impossible. He must be a relative who had inherited the count's evil aura.

She thought back to the last time she had seen her mother. Her mother had given her the precious, powerful amethyst pendant Ilona's father had gifted her on the occasion of their daughter's birth, willing Ilona the sum of her powers. She had given Ilona a pouch of gold coins for the long journey ahead and entrusted her daughter with a tradesman in a wagon with instructions to deliver her daughter to Calais, where she could get a boat to England and sail on to America. When Ilona woke up in Calais, the tradesman was gone, along with most of her gold coins. And she was alone, forced to find her way however she could, until she made passage to America. She was cold, lonely, and hungry. She missed her mother, but she knew she couldn't go back. She was on her own.

When she arrived on the Florida coast, at Casa Spirito, the reverend had welcomed her, supplied her with a house and a way to make a living. He had been her salvation. She thought she was in love with him and he with her. He had promised to leave his wife. But when he took away her daughter, her love had turned to hatred.

It was better not to think of the past.

Sometimes she thought she had only dreamed her mother. It had been so long since they had been together. Was her mother still in Hungary? Did she ever try to find her daughter? It had been ages since she'd heard that name, her real name, Ilona. She thought she'd left it behind, but her past was crashing in around her. She could feel the bitter winds of yesterday rising, making her heart quake and shattering her peace of mind.

Chapter Twenty

Gedeon took a steaming shower, soaped down, and harbored dangerous thoughts. Lurid thoughts about his gypsy queen, Marika—or was it Ilona? They had become blended in his mind. From now on, Ilona's future would be tied to his. He imagined her naked, her voluptuous body beneath his, bucking, arching, opening to him. He would take her forcefully at first, to teach her who was in charge. She had gotten too independent in all these years away from him. He'd tame her, like he tamed his horses, beat her if he had to, until her spirit was broken. And then he'd awaken her to all the pleasures he could offer her, riches beyond her wildest dreams, her body and his on a wild, sensuous ride. Immortality. He was anxious to conclude his business and spirit her away to his castle. They had so much time to make up for. Gedeon sniffed. He could still smell her lovely scent.

Toweling off, he dressed carefully in his disguise and reviewed his plan. Ilona was a formidable force, but he was stronger. She thought she was protected, but no one was safe from the Devastater.

****

Will took Juliette's arm to lead her out of the department store. "Jack and I are going to take a walk down to the Hamilton police station to have a brief chat with the local police. We need to see if they've caught wind of our suspect. Are you ladies ready to leave?"

"Will, we're not even near done shopping," Kate protested.

Jack frowned. "Do you think you will be okay here by yourselves? We shouldn't be gone more than half an hour."

Kate placed a hand on Jack's shoulder. "We'll be fine. We're going to stay right here in the store. There are people all around us. Nothing bad will happen to us."

"I think the girls need a break," Will agreed. "They were cooped up on the ship looking at mug shots for two days instead of relaxing. They need to shop."

Jack cast a doubtful eye at Kate.

"Jack, you and Will go on," Kate urged. "I don't think I could stand being in another police station. I have a huge shopping list, and we haven't even made a dent in it."

His eyes bored into Kate's. "Promise me you won't leave this store."

"I promise."

Jack and Will looked back once more, and Kate and Juliette were already riding the escalator to the children's department.

"Shopping for jewelry, china, and crystal, linens, and watches is a lot easier than trying to find a killer," said Juliette, rubbing her feet. "Although it's hard on the feet. I'm ready for a swim or a foot rub."

"But I want to show you around the local arts and crafts shops," said Kate. "I'd like to bring home some Bermuda honey, Bermuda perfume, and tasty rum cakes. But first I need to take a bathroom break. I'll meet you right back here."

"Oh, I see the cutest infant outfits," Juliette cooed. "Go on ahead. I'll wait here for you in this department."

Juliette browsed through the racks. Each baby outfit was cuter than the next. She had a lot of catching up to do in the mothering department. She'd missed Kate's childhood. She wasn't going to miss a minute of her grandchild's life. She'd start out with these cute gifts, have them wrapped and sent home as a surprise for Kate.

"May I help you?"

Juliette looked up at the tall store clerk.

"Why, yes, I'd like to have some outfits gift wrapped and sent back to Atlanta as a surprise for my daughter. She's expecting a baby."

"I'd be glad to help you with that. Show me the items you had in mind."

Juliette grabbed three outfits off the rack and placed them on the counter.

"Excellent. Now let me get your mailing information."

While Juliette was filling out the mailing form, the clerk circled around the counter, hovering over her.

"Is there anything else you need?" asked Juliette, beginning to feel uncomfortable, as she put down the pen and left the mailing form on the counter. "Let me get out my credit card." When she looked up from her purse, the clerk was right behind her.

"Ouch." Juliette rubbed her arm. "I think I've been stung. By a mosquito or a bee." She looked at her arm and then up at the clerk.

The clerk opened a wheelchair. "Here, have a seat. Let me take a look at that arm."

Juliette shook her head. "I don't need a wheelchair.

I'm fine, really—" She stumbled and went limp in the clerk's arms. Gently positioning Juliette in the chair, he grabbed the mailing form and wheeled Juliette swiftly toward the elevator.

A female store employee sporting severe tortoiseshell glasses blocked his way like a troll guarding the bridge. "Is there a problem?"

"Yes, this customer fainted. I'm going to wheel her outside for a bit of fresh air."

"Where do you work?" the woman inquired.

"I'm in menswear. I was on break and just happened by when this woman fainted."

"That was quick thinking. I'd like to report this to your supervisor, Mr.—"

"No need to call attention to me. I just did what anyone would do in this situation."

The man pressed the elevator button and wheeled Juliette into the elevator, leaving the woman to stare open-mouthed after them.

When they arrived on the ground floor, the clerk opened an umbrella, covering his face, and wheeled her out of the store. A cab was waiting, and he gave the driver instructions.

The cab driver offered to help with the wheelchair.

"I can handle it from here," said the clerk. "Stay in the cab." He lifted Juliette and settled her into the back seat, leaving the wheelchair on the sidewalk.

"Hurry. This lady needs medical attention."

Chapter Twenty-One

The baby was probably only the size of a grapefruit, but he or she (Juliette was convinced it was a girl) was already wreaking havoc on Kate's bladder. Every time she saw a water fountain, she had to go. If she took a drink of water, she had to go. If she thought about a waterfall, she had to go. And being on the ocean these past few days, well, she couldn't pass a restroom without going inside.

Kate dried her hands on a paper towel and made her way back to the children's department. She looked around for Juliette. No doubt her mother had wandered off to browse through the fine china or jewelry departments. There was so much to do and see in this store. Kate wandered through the various departments on that floor. Juliette wouldn't have left the floor without letting her know, would she?

When she couldn't find Juliette, she told herself to remain calm. Everything was all right. She returned to the children's department, and on the counter were three precious outfits. Kate picked them up and closed her eyes. Juliette had held these. Her mother's mindprints were all over the pink clothing. Although they hadn't known each other long, she had forged a strong bond with Juliette. She hadn't been able to receive a signal from the parents who raised her when they were in danger, but she was getting strong, urgent signals from Juliette. Kate's heart rate accelerated. Juliette was in trouble. She was sure of it.

She caught the attention of a woman wearing a store name badge.

"Have you seen an attractive middle-aged woman in a lavender cotton dress? She was in this department just a few minutes ago."

The sales clerk paused and tilted her head. Her eyes widened beneath her tortoiseshell glasses.

"What did she look like?"

"Like me, but about twenty years older."

"Was she in a wheelchair?"

"A wheelchair?" Kate looked puzzled. "No."

"I saw a man, a tall man, a clerk from menswear, wheeling a woman who resembled you to the elevator. He said she'd fainted and he was taking her outside for some fresh air."

"That doesn't make any sense. Juliette was fine when I left her."

Kate picked up the pink outfits. Another odor permeated the clothes. Not Juliette's. An evil aura.

"Could you describe the store clerk? You said he was tall?"

"Very tall, as a matter of fact. He said he worked in menswear."

"I need to find that man. Where's menswear?"

"I'm the store manager. I'll take you down there. I didn't recognize him, so he must be new, or maybe a temporary transfer from one of our other stores on the island." Kate followed the manager down the escalator to the menswear department. The manager went to a sales clerk and held a brief conversation. Then she returned to Kate.

"There's no one who fits that description who works in menswear."

"If the man wheeled her outside, then they're probably gone by now, but I need to check."

"Do you think something happened to your sister?"

Kate choked. "She's not my sister. She's my mother. And yes, I'm afraid—" Kate couldn't continue. She was afraid to verbalize her worst fears.

The manager followed Kate out the store's entrance on Front Street.

Kate almost tripped over an abandoned wheelchair. She touched the seat of the chair. Juliette had definitely been here. Her aura was totally overpowered by a second stream sense. It was the man from the ship's gallery. The man who had stolen the paintings. The man who had most probably killed the auctioneer. The man who now had Juliette.

Kate stilled her hands and tried not to panic. Jack. She needed Jack. Her hands flew to the phone in her purse. But before she could make the call, Jack and Will strode up to the store's entrance.

"You ladies done shopping? I thought we'd agreed that you would remain in the store."

Kate pushed her hand against Jack's chest.

"It's Juliette. She's vanished."

Chapter Twenty-Two

Juliette felt woozy. Her head ached. Her heart raced. Her throat was as parched and dry as cotton candy. But the taste in her mouth was anything but sweet. Bile threatened to rise in her throat. She raised a hand to steady herself and keep from falling, before she realized she was already lying down. On a bed. She tried to get up, but she couldn't move. Was she back on the ship? It felt like the bed was swaying.

A deep melodic voice wafted into her consciousness.

"Good. My sleeping beauty is awake."

Juliette's vision swam into focus and she looked up. It was him. The man on the ship. What had happened to the store clerk? The last thing she remembered was a pinch in her arm. She wanted to rub the sore spot, but her hands were—tied with rope. She struggled against the bonds. Her legs were unencumbered, but her dress had slid up her thighs and her panties were visible.

The man laughed, a deep, booming chuckle. "I see you're confused. That's only natural."

"You drugged me," Juliette accused.

"Only a slight pinch of sedative to calm you down."

The man reached down and smoothed Juliette's brow, touched her hair, touched her thighs lightly before lowering the fabric of her dress.

Juliette shrank away as far as the ropes would allow. Away from his smell. His evil aura.

"Calm down. You're still a little skittish. We'll take care of that. Perhaps another shot?"

The man's lips curled in a smirk.

"No." She thought she had stated her response emphatically but it came out as a squeak. Her strength was sapped.

"The man in the store."

"That was a disguise. Brilliant, don't you think? You didn't recognize me."

"You're the auctioneer from the gallery."

"Very perceptive."

"Where am I? Are we back on the ship?"

"No, I'm afraid not. That ship has sailed, or it will be sailing tonight. If you cooperate, your friends will be on it. And if you don't, well, then, I shudder to think what accident might befall them. Especially that adorable, delectable daughter of yours. The one carrying your grandchild?"

Juliette tried to wriggle out of the bonds, but they dug deeper into her hands. "How—?"

"You told me. Remember those cute pink outfits you picked out? And you gave me your mailing address, so I know exactly where you and your family live."

"Do not harm Kate, or I'll—"

The man lifted the amethyst pendant from Juliette's chest and twisted the chain.

"This is the source of your power, and now it's mine. I choose to let you wear it for now, but it's of no use to you in your current state. You're helpless, I'm afraid."

Juliette tried to break free of the ropes, but her body was as loose as gelatin.

He released the chain and skimmed his fingers lightly over Juliette's breasts, then rubbed his thumb over Juliette's lower lip. She turned away in disgust. Her heart pounded in her chest. The amethyst amulet glowed hot.

He fixed his gaze on her exposed legs, then turned and walked to a green wing chair, where he sat, his hands steepled like some satisfied godfather, and continued to leer at her.

"Plenty of time for that later, after we've gotten better acquainted," the man said, his voice as smooth as honey. "I'm Gedeon, by the way."

Juliette was silent.

"I see that name means nothing to you. You don't remember me. You were just a little girl then. Do you remember the castle in Hungary, Ilona? If, and only if, you're cooperative, I can tell you about your mother."

Juliette angled to sit up in the bed, but her dress slipped higher on her thighs until she was totally exposed.

"You want to learn about what happened to her, yes?"

Juliette nodded.

"I've been waiting to tell you about the beautiful Marika. Queen of the castle. Or she could have been. But now you can take her place. You look exactly like her. Marika." He sighed.

The man was obviously crazy. He was confusing her with her mother. More than anything, she wanted to find out about her mother. If her mother was still alive, then she wanted to go to her by any means available.

Juliette scanned the room.

"Where are we? Are we still in Bermuda?"

"We're in a guest house that belongs to an acquaintance of mine. It's a stunning view. It's a shame we don't have time to enjoy it." He stared at her breasts and rubbed his beard. We'll be sailing to Europe this evening."

"But our ship is heading for America."

"We're not taking the cruise ship. I've hired a luxury motor yacht."

"My daughter will find me. She and Jack and Will would never leave without me."

"Your husband Will? I know that marriage is a sham." The man seemed to know everything about her. "Ilona, do you know how many cottages, suites, apartments, hotels, inns, and bed-and-breakfasts there on the island, not to mention private clubs and residences? Finding us would be like finding a needle in a haystack, as I believe the Americans are fond of saying. And besides, I've left a note on the wheelchair saying that you weren't feeling well and you've returned to the ship. By the time they realize you're not aboard, we'll be long gone, and so will they."

Juliette shivered, and her hands shook. Then she calmed. She couldn't afford to be afraid or angry. She had to focus on a plan of escape.

"I have no doubt you're a capable woman. I recall that you killed your lover, the Reverend Carter Coulter, but please don't make the mistake of underestimating me, Ilona. I've been planning this for a long time. The heist, at least. Our encounter was serendipitous. We were meant to be together. And we will be. I have endless resources at my disposal."

Juliette's eyes widened. Was the man a mind reader? How did he know so much about her? Perhaps he did have hidden powers.

"Our meeting was fated. Surely you don't think it was a coincidence. Now get some rest. We have a long journey ahead. And I need to finish packing. Don't worry about clothing. You won't need any on the yacht, and we can buy you whatever you need once we arrive."

Gedeon got up from the chair and began studying a stack of paintings. Then he packed them carefully into a canvas suitcase.

So Gedeon was the thief, and she was a loose end that needed to be tied up.

"Did you kill that man in the gallery?"

Gedeon turned to her and rubbed his fingers against his lips.

"I might as well come clean, since there's no one you can tell. You can yell as loud as you wish. There's no one around. And once I get you back in the castle, you won't be receiving visitors. So rest up. You're going to need your strength."

Chapter Twenty-Three

"Jack, you have to do something. Find her. She's in trouble. I can feel it." Kate touched the back of the wheelchair and shivered.

"Will, call the police," Jack instructed, glancing down at the seat of the wheelchair. "Wait, Juliette left us a note."

"What does it say?" Will asked, agitated.

"It says she's tired and she went back to the ship. She'll see us onboard."

Will relaxed, expelling a breath in relief. "I'm so glad she's okay."

Jack exhaled. "Let's get back to the ship. It's going to leave this evening anyway."

"Juliette is not on the ship. She's somewhere on this island."

"Kate, you saw the note. Juliette went back to the ship."

Kate refused to accept his words. Instead, she reached out and took the note from Jack and examined it. "This is not Juliette's handwriting."

Jack shrugged. "It makes sense that your mother would return to the ship. She knows the ship is pulling out of port tonight. She'd want to get back. Speaking of which, we need to be getting back to the ship ourselves."

"Not without my mother." Kate was insistent. "I

think someone meant us to find the note, to put us off track."

"Well, if Juliette was wheeled out in the wheelchair, our suspect could only have left here by cab. Unless he's a resident, which is unlikely, he can't drive in Bermuda, so he must have taken a taxi. Will, have the police check with cabs that left Front Street within the past hour, and find out their final destination."

Will pulled out his cell phone.

Kate's hands shook. Final destination sounded so, well, final. If the man in the gallery was a killer, then he wouldn't hesitate to kill Juliette. She had just found her mother. She didn't want to lose her. She needed her, especially now that she was bringing a new life into the world. But why would he want to hurt Juliette? Why did he single her out? He had his stolen art. Wasn't that enough? Maybe Juliette had recognized him in the store and he'd had to dispose of her?

Jack put his arms around Kate. "Don't worry. We'll find her. Your mother is a very resourceful woman. She saved my life once, remember? If he has her, he doesn't know what he's in for."

"Jack, I refuse to just stand here helplessly. I want to find her. I can track down serial killers. Why can't I save my own mother?"

"You look beat, Kate. Too much stress is not good for the baby. Let's sit down on this bench. I know you can't work well in these conditions."

Jack took Kate's hand and led her to a covered bus bench. He went to a street vendor and purchased a cold bottle of water and handed it to Kate, then pulled out his phone and started making calls.

After a long drink of cold water, Kate placed the bottle beside her on the bench, closed her eyes, and focused all her energy on trying to locate Juliette. Bermuda was a relatively small island. Surely she could pick up a signal. The day was so beautiful, it didn't seem like anything bad could happen here in paradise. But evil knew no boundaries—day or night, balmy weather or stormy—evil took root in the unlikeliest of places and at the unlikeliest of times.

Kate massaged her head, feeling the onslaught of one of her mega-headaches, which meant she was on the right track, the track of evil. She persevered because she would do anything to find her mother. She blocked off the sounds from the street, the chatter between shoppers on Front Street, Jack's voice on the phone trying to track down any clue to explain Juliette's disappearance.

In her mind, Kate saw a castle, atop a rocky outcrop, a river flowing around it. The structure was in a state of disrepair, but inside she viewed the riches of tapestries and antique furniture and artwork. Paintings by the Old Masters, from the period of the Renaissance, French Impressionists, work by artists she recognized, artwork that had never been in any museum. Priceless paintings beyond compare. And a painting in the center of the room of—was that Juliette? It was a portrait of someone who looked just like Juliette. None of this was making any sense.

Down a stone stairwell, there was a dungeon, cold and dark, and a skeleton chained to a post. Kate shivered even as she looked up at the sun overhead. Obviously she was getting interfering signals. This castle was someplace in Scotland or Ireland, or maybe

Romania? No, Hungary. Near the Transylvania border.

Kate put her hand to her forehead and pressed against her eye. She could hear screams coming from the dungeon, a woman's screams. What did this have to do with Juliette?

Kate refocused. That was another murder in another time. She was back in Bermuda. She summoned up the image of Juliette's amethyst amulet. That was always a way to reach her mother. She saw the amulet, followed by a vision of Juliette, hands tied, on a bed. She called out to Jack—but where was that room? She scanned the background. They were in a yellow mansion on the ocean. A historic colonial home, from the looks of it, probably centuries old, with an old-fashioned verandah.

"Kate, did you see something?"

Kate rubbed her forehead.

"You have another one of your headaches."

"I'll get over it. I saw Juliette."

"How about if I go back and check the ship," Will said. "Then you and Kate can follow up any leads in the city."

"Why don't you call the captain, Will? Find out if she really did return to the ship. They should have a record, if she scanned her ID card on the way onboard."

"Great idea, Kate." Will dialed the captain's number. He spoke a few sentences, and when he hung up his face was ashen.

"She never returned. She's not aboard the ship. She'd have had plenty of time to get back there by now. That means she's still out here somewhere. If I have to search every boat, every hotel room, every house on this damned island, I will."

Jack raised his brows and looked at Will. "I can understand why Kate and I need to find Juliette. But there's no one around. You don't have to pretend to be worried."

Will's face hardened. He had no psychic powers, no amethyst amulet. Just a fierce desire to find Juliette. "I'm in love with her, Jack. Now let's go find my wife."

Jack and Will bombarded Kate with questions. Questions she couldn't answer.

"All I can see is that she is tied up on a bed, in an historic yellow mansion overlooking the ocean. She's alive. She's alive." Kate blew out a breath. "And there was a man, the man on the ship, but he was just a shadow. He's tall and dressed in black. He's—" Kate shook her head.

"He's what, Kate?" Jack placed a comforting hand on Kate's shoulder.

"Some kind of a vampire, I think."

Will heaved a sigh. "Kate, we're wasting valuable time. There's no such thing as vampires."

Kate bit her bottom lip and rubbed her forehead. "I'm just telling you what I saw."

"This is unbelievable," Will shouted. "So what you're saying is that there was a vampire loose on our cruise ship?"

Kate moderated her voice. "I don't know if he's a real vampire. He's covered from head to toe in black. Vampires can't go out in the sun, you know. That's why they can't leave that house."

"Kate. Do you know how you sound? Jack, you're not buying this, are you? I can't call the police and tell them they're looking for a vampire."

"Maybe he just thinks he's a vampire," Jack

reasoned.

Kate's eyes rolled back in her head, and she fell forward into Jack's arms.

"Christ, something strange is going on. Something unworldly. I don't know what it is, but we have to hold out hope. Kate says she's still alive."

"But who knows for how long?" Will punched his fist into his hand.

Jack made a call, then turned to Will. "I've got the police out looking everywhere. If she's on the island, we'll find her."

Chapter Twenty-Four

Juliette awoke and tried to move her hands. They were numb. Memories of the past few hours came rushing back. No, this wasn't a dream. Gedeon must have drugged her again to keep her quiet.

"Marika, you're awake. Good." Gedeon glided over to the bed. He tested the restraints and seemed satisfied they were tight enough. "It won't be long now. As soon as it turns dark, we'll be on our way."

"Why do we have to wait until dark?"

"I think you know the answer to that question, my love. I only operate in the dark. I have a condition—sensitive skin. It's hereditary. I shun sunlight. Don't you remember?"

Juliette tried to sit up. She glanced at the looming presence above her. She was alone in a room with a madman who thought she was her mother. A delusional man who thought he was a vampire. A man who was determined to kidnap her and take her back to his castle. Okay, she could play along with him.

"Are you going to bite me?" She was half afraid he might, that he might follow through on her suggestion.

"You're afraid I'm going to turn you." Gedeon paused and ran a finger lightly up and down Juliette's neck, pausing at the pulse point. "I have strong appetites."

Juliette shrank back and managed to move into a

sitting position, trying not to show her fear. And she could see by the crazy light in Gedeon's eyes that he was aroused.

"All will be revealed when we return home."

Gedeon touched the amethyst amulet around Juliette's neck. It glowed.

"Don't be afraid. I'm tempted to take a taste of you, but when I take you, you'll hunger for me just as I have hungered for you all of these years. Don't pretend to be innocent. I know all about the years you spent with the reverend, your *protector*. The older, wiser man. I'm sure he taught you well. Lessons I'm sure I'll appreciate. And then there's the sheriff. I can only imagine what you two were doing in your suite. You're damaged goods, but I am willing to overlook that. And yes, I will turn you. I made that mistake with Marika. If I had joined our blood, she'd still be with me today. But she chose to—"

"What about my mother? What happened to her?"

"Hush, my love." Gedeon placed his fingertips on Juliette's lips. "In due time."

Juliette's body began to shake. She was all alone. There was no one around to help her. She had to depend on herself. The ship had surely sailed, and with it her family and Will and all hopes of rescue. Will. She'd been fighting him all along, but he was a good man. She could fall in love with a man like that. What did she know of love? All the men she had ever met had wanted to control her or use her. She'd never really known love until she met Will. And now she'd never get a chance to explore that love with him.

She knew Gedeon could not remove the amulet. No one could. He wanted it, wanted her power, but she would have to give it willingly. She had to take a chance. Maybe if she riled him he would make a mistake.

"You know I am not Marika."

Gedeon rose from the bed and growled. "You are whoever I wish you to be. When I bed you, you will sing to my tune and play your role, or you'll go to your grave, like your mother."

Juliette strained against the bonds.

"You said you'd tell me about my mother. She's not alive?"

Gedeon paced the room impatiently. "I'm done talking. Now we're about to leave. Do I need to sedate you again, or will you come willingly? If you don't, you know what will happen to Kate."

Juliette's mind wandered to a time when her mother had sacrificed herself to protect her daughter. Now Juliette would willingly carry on that tradition.

"I will cooperate. Now untie me."

Gedeon seemed satisfied with that answer.

"You're ready to dispense with this pretense? You used to burn at my touch. Don't you remember, Marika?"

The vampire's hold on reality was unraveling at a rapid rate.

"I do," Juliette whispered.

"And you will again." Gedeon loosened her hands and lifted her out of the bed. Juliette's arms ached. Her body ached. Her strength had been depleted.

All the stories she'd heard about vampires were one-sided. What would happen if you bit a vampire? Or made him angry? Would he bite back?

When he leaned in to steal a kiss, she took a bite

out of Gedeon's arm.

"You little bitch," he yelled and dropped her unceremoniously on the carpeted floor. Juliette scrambled out of the room and locked the door behind her, sealing off the vampire and his monstrous rage.

Chapter Twenty-Five

"We've got several reports of cabs dropping off passengers in front of private residences, which is suspicious because Bermuda residents can drive, so why would they need to take a cab?"

"Let's check them out," Will said, straining to be on the way, like a starving hound.

"We need to wait for the police car. They know the island. We don't. We may need backup."

At that moment a local police car pulled up, and the driver emerged.

"I'm Captain Smith. I'm here to provide any assistance you need. There's room for everyone in the car."

Kate and Jack got in the back seat, and Will sat in front with the police captain.

"Okay, we have several addresses to check out. One is at a yellow private home in Hamilton. That's the closest."

"Does it have an ocean view?" Kate asked.

"No, primarily garden views, but very lovely. The wife and I—"

"They're not there," Kate stated abruptly. "We're looking for a yellow mansion on a cliff overlooking the ocean." A clear picture of the house burned in her mind.

Captain Smith checked his list. "Well, there's only one on the list that it could possibly be, then. The cab driver said his passenger was asleep in the back seat. He offered to help with her wheelchair, but the man she was with left it in the doorway on Front Street."

"That's them!" Will shouted. "Let's go."

"Well, then, we have a problem. That's a private residence. We can't just barge in there."

"We can ring the doorbell, can't we?" Will reasoned.

"We can. I'll radio ahead for backup. The gentleman who owns that property is a big muckety-muck."

Jack piped in from the back seat. "Is he local?"

"He's a British citizen with fingers in all sorts of pies. He's connected, that's for sure. Don't want to rile him. He won't abide us banging on his door unannounced."

"I don't care what he will or won't abide. If I have to break the door down, I will." Will was steaming in the front seat.

Jack placed his hand on Will's shoulder. "Calm down. We're going to find her."

Kate closed her eyes and focused. Juliette was running, running for her life. Doors locked. Doors splintered. Long arms getting closer, closer to her neck. Juliette clutched her amulet, praying for strength. Now she was outside, running under a moon gate in the garden, breath coming in precious gulps, running around trees, closer and closer to the cliff and the ocean's edge. Waves crashed below. The first star blinked in the darkening sky. The moon rose. Dusk. The man wanted to give chase. But something was holding him back. He was waiting until nightfall.

Juliette bolted forward breathlessly, trying to

outpace the monster. She was scared, shaking, shoeless. There was nowhere to go. The man was right behind her, his shoes pounding the grass. She didn't have to look back to know she was cornered.

"Hurry," Kate whispered.

"Kate, did you say something?" Jack stared at his wife, in her trancelike state.

"Hurry."

"How much longer?" Will demanded, drumming his fists on the dashboard.

"Five to ten minutes, no more." The police car sped around a dry stone wall that leaned away from the road.

"If I go any faster, we'll all be killed."

****

Juliette's heart hammered in her chest. Clutching the amulet, she prayed—to her mother's soul, to a higher power, to whoever was out there, whoever would listen. She stopped short. If she went any farther, she'd end up splattered on the rocks below. Maybe that would be preferable to the fate Gedeon had in mind for her. But she wanted to live, at any cost. She wanted to see Kate again. She skidded to a halt and managed to swerve to the right. Gedeon's steps closed the space between them. She felt his fingers reaching for her hair, but she was no longer in front of him. The momentum carried him forward, but he stopped himself before he went over the cliff. If he did go over the cliff, could he really fly?

****

A flash of purple fabric appeared to his right. Gedeon pursued it. Did the little fool think she could outrun him? He was a hawk. She was his prey. He was lightning fast and super strong. She was earthbound. He was invincible. But she persisted in playing her dreary cat-and-mouse games. He'd have to punish her when they got back to the castle. He bit his bottom lip. There were endless instruments of torture at his disposal and, of course, the dungeon, where her mother had met her end. He wouldn't make that mistake again. Starvation had seemed like a good idea at the time, but he had overestimated Marika's stamina and stubbornness.

But punishment would have to wait. They had a schedule to keep, and they needed to make it to the yacht. The limo he'd hired to take them to the wharf was idling in front of the house. His bags and the remainder of the paintings were already loaded in the car. Perhaps Juliette had hoped he would leave her behind. She had run now toward the front of the house, seeking salvation.

"Help me," she pleaded. He heard her voice rise to a crescendo. Her hands were pounding on the window on the driver's side of the dark stretch limousine. "Someone is after me."

"Get in," the driver said, obligingly. Juliette got into the back seat and doubled over, struggling to catch her breath, thankful to be rescued.

Gedeon smiled. Always expect the unexpected. While Juliette's head was down, he slipped into the limo next to her, locked the doors and signaled to the driver to take off.

****

When Juliette raised her head, the shock was etched on her face. She clutched at her heart. She had escaped right into the devil's tentacles. She saw Gedeon lift the syringe from his jacket pocket and felt it sink into her shoulder. The last thing she remembered was his smile as she slumped over into his lap.

****

Gedeon smiled as he watched Ilona—or was it Marika?—fall forward. He stroked her hair, winding his fingers into the beautiful mass of black curls. If only they were alone and Ilona had not been so obstinate.

The limo driver knew where to go. They were mere minutes from the wharf.

Chapter Twenty-Six

"This is it," Kate exclaimed. "This is the house."

The police car slowed to a stop on the circular driveway, and the occupants piled out. They ran up the steps of the welcoming arms staircase to the front door of the magnificent Tucker's Town stone residence with its pale yellow walls and traditional Bermuda stepped roof.

The police captain knocked on the door.

No answer.

Then he rang the bell.

"This isn't a damn social call," Will bellowed. "Break down the door."

"This is Bermuda cedar. It can't be easily broken."

"Then break a window."

"That's uncivilized."

"You think I care how it looks? Try the back door."

The officer started around to the back, and Will, Jack, and Kate followed. The house was large and heavily landscaped, and darkness and unfamiliarity with the property impeded their progress.

He entered a garden, walked up to the back door, and jiggled the handle. The door was open. He turned the handle, walked in, and raised his weapon. "If they were here, they must have left in a hurry."

Will nearly bumped into the officer as he rushed in and looked around, while the officer did a room-by-room check. Nothing seemed out of place. No sign of anything amiss, until he got to the bedroom. "I smell Juliette's perfume."

"Juliette was definitely here," Kate confirmed.

Will turned on the light and was confronted with a horrifying scene on the four-poster bed. A scene such as he had processed before in his career as a sheriff. But this time it was personal. He pointed to the bed but couldn't speak.

Ropes were tied to the bedposts, ropes that had obviously held Juliette captive.

The officer walked into the bedroom and frowned at the sight of the ropes. "I've checked the entire house. There's no one here."

"I saw her in this bed, tied up. She was here, I'm sure." Kate touched her hands to her stomach and shivered.

Will pounded his fist against the wall and shouted, "Then where is she?"

"Jack, look," Kate said, pointing to two paintings on the wall and walking closer to inspect them. "The missing Monets. These were two of the paintings I saw in the gallery on the ship."

"Are you absolutely sure?"

"Jack, there's no mistaking Monets. These are authentic. Whoever lives here must have purchased them from our art thief. And now he's missing."

"Well, he had no way of knowing we were on to them, so they must have been following a plan," Jack reasoned. "No need to go to another location on the island if he felt safe here. Except it was strange that they left the back door open. Maybe they had to flee in a hurry. There's no way off the island except by boat."

"He wouldn't take the cruise ship, because he'd know we were looking for him," Jack reasoned, turning to the police captain. "Could he have chartered a vessel?"

"I'll make a call and check that out and contact another officer to secure the scene here."

What no one was saying out loud was—the crime scene. No evidence of a crime committed here, except possibly a depraved act. The man would have had plenty of time to do what he pleased with Juliette.

Jack put his arm around Kate. "Meanwhile, I'll contact the captain and alert him that they might try to sneak back on the ship."

"What about the paintings? We can't just leave these here. We need to return these to the French government, get them back to a museum or trace them back to their rightful owners before they disappear again."

"We will," Jack assured her.

"I don't care about the paintings," Will objected. "We can't just stand here and do nothing. We need to find Juliette. Let's go to where the boats are docked."

The police captain laughed. "This island is surrounded by water. Almost everyone on Bermuda has a boat. They could conceivably leave from anywhere, the wharf on the harbor, a private club, a private residence. We have no idea what type of boat they're on or what their destination could be."

"Could they possibly be headed for Europe?" Kate suggested. "Maybe to Hungary?"

"It's as good a hunch as any," said Captain Smith. "We can start out with the yachts." The officer made a call. "Let's head to the wharf at Hamilton. That's most likely where they'll be."

The four headed for the front of the house, where they piled into the police car. The officer circled around and headed back on the road to Hamilton.

Chapter Twenty-Seven

"Help me get her out of the car," Gedeon ordered. He lifted Juliette by her head and shoulders, and the driver lifted her feet. Passed out, her body felt like dead weight. They boarded the yacht and walked down to one of the bedrooms below and tossed Juliette onto the bed. Gedeon watched for any signs of movement and, satisfied, saw none.

"Get my luggage stowed," said Gedeon. "I'll take the big package myself."

Gedeon handed the driver a hundred-dollar bill. "Now, not a word to anyone. If anyone asks, you didn't see me or the woman. If I find out otherwise, you'll be sorry."

The driver held up his hands. "I never saw you." He scurried off the ship like a rat.

A man in uniform introduced himself. "I'm the captain. Welcome aboard. The chef will have dinner ready in about an hour. Meanwhile, we'll have some appetizers brought out for you and the lady."

Gedeon scowled. "The lady is rather ill, and she gets seasick, I'm afraid. She'll be spending most of the trip in her cabin. So she's not to be disturbed. She's heavily medicated, so I don't want to take a chance of having her on deck. She might slip into the ocean. I'm not hungry."

The captain nodded. "Well, if that's everything,

we'll be setting sail within minutes."

Gedeon carried his paintings into the second cabin, opened the Murphy bed, carefully placed the package on the mattress, and folded it into the wall. Unfortunately, he'd had to cut this trip short and so would be bringing back several of the paintings he had hoped to sell. He didn't want any of the crew snooping around. He'd be spending the trip in Juliette's cabin, so they'd be sharing a bed. No need for a bed of his own. But in case Juliette woke up, he didn't want her to have access to his priceless package.

He walked into Juliette's room. She was still asleep. She hadn't eaten anything since he'd taken her this afternoon, but leaving her in a weakened state fit his plans. If she was good, he would feed her a few morsels, maybe offer her some water in return for—he stopped himself before he got too excited. Plenty of time for that once they were under way. She could either spend the voyage tied up and hungry, or they could be lovers. The decision was hers. He hoped she had better sense than her mother. Making love on a boat at sea was sublime, and it was a long voyage. The next time the sedative wore off, he might add something extra to the mix, just to get her in the mood. Some women needed help jumpstarting their desires. He had a lot to offer, and the sooner she realized her future was with him, the better it would be for her.

He didn't want to have to gag her, but even on this large yacht people would be able to hear her screams, and he couldn't afford to draw any attention to himself. She would be out for several more hours, and when she came to, he'd be there to quiet her and smother her screams, with a gag or with his mouth; it would be her choice. He anchored her wrists—for her own protection. She would still be listless when she woke. He couldn't take the chance that she would wander about the ship and accidentally fall overboard.

He breathed in her alluring scent and studied her body as he sat beside her on the bed. She was irresistible—beautiful and curvy, a heady combination. He ventured a touch to the tips of her voluptuous breasts. He could easily slip off her panties. No, first things first. He would go out on deck, make small talk with the captain. Then, after they were under way, he'd come back to the cabin to see how his captive was faring. See if she had grown any more receptive to his attentions. She would if she knew what was good for her.

Gedeon was looking forward to walking the deck and breathing in the cool night air in the shadow of the stars. He desired to spend as much of the night outside as possible, to recharge, and the daylight hours occupied in Juliette's cabin. She would soon learn his daily rhythms and adjust to his requirements. Sunlight was overrated. He contemplated the wonderful life they'd have together. He couldn't wait to share it with her. She would be his Persephone, his possession in the bowels of Hades or within the walls of his castle, at night; free to wander about in the daylight, but under heavy guard.

Of course she had been hesitant, at first. That was only natural. He'd half forgiven her already for trying to escape. He believed in second chances. He had looked for her for half a lifetime. She needed time to grow used to his touch, to his lips on her body, before he entered her. He was throbbing. He couldn't wait to taste her. Would she be as ripe as Marika? Could he tame her like he'd failed to tame Marika? He would certainly have fun trying.

He left his sleeping beauty, calm and peaceful and happy. Was that a faint smile on her lips? Was she dreaming of him? In the end, her body would betray her, just like Marika's had.

Gedeon tiptoed out the door, so as not to wake his sleeping princess, and went up the wooden stairs to the upper deck to stretch and seek the moonlight.

Chapter Twenty-Eight

The police captain hung up his phone. "We've got several large yachts docked at the wharf. We'll have to board them one by one."

"There's no time." Will jiggled his silver handcuffs relentlessly.

Jack's firm hand calmed Will. "Kate, concentrate. Can you see Juliette? Can you help us find her?"

Kate closed her eyes and leaned back in her seat. Her face grimaced in pain, and she clutched the armrest.

"Kate," Will prompted.

"She's concentrating. Give her a chance. These things can't be rushed."

Blocking out all noises, the constant lap of the water against the dock, disembodied voices, she saw—not Juliette but the man, Wade Russell. But he wasn't a man. He was a monster, cloaked in darkness, clothed from head to toe in black. His white teeth glistened in a mouth twisted into a satisfied snarl. He was here, but on which boat? She made out the name, *The Marika*, and the horizontal tricolored red, white, and blue flag with the Croatian coat of arms in the center. She felt Juliette's presence, but her mother was asleep, thankfully passed out in oblivion.

"*The Marika*," Kate mouthed, her throat parched, her head pounding.

Jack looked up at the captain. "Could that be the name of a ship?"

The captain consulted his computer. "Not registered in Bermuda. There is a ship called *The Marika* registered in Croatia. That's a popular place to charter yachts, especially for owners who live in landlocked countries like Hungary."

"Let's go." Will was out the door.

"You don't have any jurisdiction here," the captain said. "You have no authority to carry a gun. Without a weapon, what can you do?"

"I have my bare hands," Will answered. "And I'm going to rip this murderer apart."

Will raced up and down the dock until he spotted a sleek black yacht called *The Marika*. Jack and the captain followed.

The yacht was about to pull out of its slip.

"Hold on," Will shouted to the man unmooring the boat. "We're with the police, and we need to ask you some questions."

A man clad in black sat next to the captain's chair, and when he saw Will and the others approaching, he fled down the steps, calling out, "Set sail, immediately."

The captain, garbed in white, approached the group.

"What's this about? We need to get under way."

"What's the hurry?" The police captain stepped in front of Will. "How many passengers do you have on board?"

"In addition to the crew, two. The owner and a female passenger."

"Where is she?" Will demanded.

"Below deck. She's not feeling well. Haven't seen much of her since she boarded."

"It's her. It's got to be her," Will pressed. "How did she look when she arrived?"

"They carried her in because she was on medication."

"He's drugged her, the bastard. I'm going after him."

"She wasn't drugged," the captain of the vessel insisted. "She's seasick. She's staying below, confined to her cabin."

"I've been with this woman on a cruise for almost a week, and she showed no signs of seasickness. Something fishy is going on."

Three large black crows landed on the yacht's railing and started squawking.

Will pointed to the birds. "They're Juliette's crows. They're trying to warn us."

The yacht's captain scratched his head. "That's strange. You don't usually see crows out here, and never at night."

"It's a sign," said Will. "Where is this woman you're talking about? Show us her room."

"The count is down there with her now. He asked that they not be disturbed."

The vein on Will's neck began to pulse.

"The records say this ship is registered to a Mr. Nagy Gedeon?" asked the police captain.

The captain of *The Marika* nodded in confirmation. "Yes, that's right. Count Nagy."

"We're going to need to interview the count and see his passenger."

"I have my instructions," the captain insisted.

Captain Smith was equally forceful. "I will impound this boat if you don't cooperate. Permission to board."

The ship's captain threw up his hands and ordered one of his crew to re-secure the boat to the dock.

Will was first to jump aboard, followed by Jack and then Captain Smith. They took the wooden steps that wound down into the bowels of the boat at a furious pace.

"Ilona. We have to go."

Juliette stirred, her mind in a fog. The man was shaking her awake, slapping her. He carried a package and was untying her from the bed.

"Where are you taking me?"

"Don't ask any questions." He grabbed her hands and tried to pull her to her feet, but she stumbled, too weak to keep her balance.

He lifted her up, trying to balance the package at the same time. He ran up the stairs and plowed into Will, who almost knocked the breath out of him. Thrusting Juliette into Will's arms, he clutched the package and ran by the police captain and right into Jack.

Jack grabbed his hands and wrested the package out of them.

"My paintings," cried the man.

Jack tossed the package to Kate.

"Those are private property." The man scowled.

"Somebody's private property, but not yours," Kate accused. Will ran up the stairs.

"How's Juliette?" Jack asked.

"She's foggy and shaky and dehydrated. The ropes left some bruises. She's resting comfortably in the cabin. She'll need a doctor." Will walked over to the fugitive in Jack's iron grip.

"Is this the man?"

Jack nodded and asked Captain Smith to call for an ambulance.

Will drew out his handcuffs, grabbed the man's hands, and cuffed him to the yacht's steering wheel. At the touch of the cuffs, the man's wrists began to sizzle, and Will's captive screamed in agony.

"Take off the handcuffs! The silver is burning my hands!"

"What are you talking about?"

Juliette climbed up the stairs. "Will, he's a vampire. Silver burns him."

"You don't actually believe that, do you?"

"I don't know what to believe."

"I thought vampires were afraid of the sun."

"And silver."

Kate ran over to Juliette and wrapped her in an embrace. "Juliette—Mom, are you all right?"

"A little hungry and thirsty and sore. This man kidnapped me and drugged me and threatened me and starved me."

"Let's see if vampires can bleed."

Will pulled back his fist and punched the man squarely in the nose. Bone crunched and blood flowed out of his nose.

"I know you're a beast, but I don't believe you're a vampire. Either way, I'd love to put a wooden stake through your dark heart."

The man wouldn't stop screaming, and the crows were making a riotous noise in concert. They flew over to Juliette and landed, one on each hand and one on her shoulder.

Juliette soothed them, and when they were quiet they flew off.

Will hugged Juliette. "I thought I'd lost you."

"I'm okay now that you're here." Will kissed her tenderly and led her over to the captain's chair. "Rest here until the ambulance comes."

Kate brought the brown paper package over to Jack. "These are the paintings we've been looking for. This artwork is priceless. The Monets are gone, but they're hanging in the yellow house in Tucker's Town. I think we have our proof. "

Jack turned to the handcuffed man. "We have some questions to ask you."

"Take these handcuffs off, and I'll answer you."

Will stayed Jack's hand. "The cuffs stay. In fact, I'm going to keep you cuffed until sunrise, and we'll put you to the ultimate test. If you disintegrate, then we'll know you really were a vampire."

The man howled. "You can't do that."

"I can and I will, and I'll enjoy watching you burn, Gideon."

"Gedeon."

"Whatever."

"Did you kill the gallery auctioneer on the cruise ship?" Jack asked.

"I won't tell you anything until you remove these handcuffs."

"The cuffs stay on." Will was adamant.

"I paid him to take the paintings aboard ship. I had pre-sold two in Bermuda and was planning to sell the rest in the States, until he came around asking for more money to keep quiet. He went back on our agreement, so, yes, I killed him, and I was going to throw his body overboard until these women came sniffing around the gallery."

"Where did you get these paintings?"

"I own them. They've been in my castle in Hungary for decades. They're family heirlooms."

"These paintings were stolen by the Nazis from museums all over Europe," Kate interrupted. "They've been missing since the war."

"The Nazis stored them in our castle when they occupied our town. When they fled, they left the paintings behind. They became my property."

"They belong to the world," Kate disagreed.

"Whenever I needed money, I sold them off, one by one. The private buyers didn't hesitate to pay our price, nor did they return them to the museums they were stolen from."

Will was curious. "You lived in a castle?"

Juliette answered. "Yes, he claims to have lived in a castle in Hungary near the Transylvania border. My mother and I lived right outside the castle gates. The last time I saw my mother, she was walking toward the castle and she told me to leave. She said the man who lived there—the count—wanted me. I know now she was sacrificing herself to save me."

"Is that true?" Jack demanded.

The man looked at his blistering wrists.

"If you'll remove the handcuffs—"

"Don't remove them, Will," Juliette warned. "Vampires are very crafty. His wrists will heal as soon as you remove the cuffs."

"Juliette, he's got you fooled," Will said. "He's only a man. An evil man. But he's not a vampire."

Juliette faced the vampire. "Where is my mother? You promised you'd tell me what happened to her."

"Answer the lady, or the cuffs stay on." Will wrinkled his nose at the smell of burning flesh. "You can rot in hell, for all I care. Hell is where you belong."

Gedeon laughed. "Your mother was a most beautiful woman, like yourself. I desired her, even loved her, but your mother refused my affections. I offered to marry her. But she refused me. So I locked her in the dungeon until she was ready to give herself to me. Marika was a stubborn woman. I starved her, beat her, tortured her, but still she refused. She's still there, standing in chains, or rather her bones are still there."

Juliette whimpered, and tears streamed down her cheeks. She covered her face. "And were you planning to do the same to me?"

"I knew you would learn to love me."

Juliette spat. "I could never love you."

Kate went to Juliette and held up a painting of a beautiful woman, a gypsy, dressed in red, dancing around a campfire, with a young girl looking on.

"Is that you?"

Juliette touched the painting. "That's my mother, your grandmother, and the little girl in the picture is me. He must have had her portrait painted. He thought I was Marika. He kept calling me by her name."

"That painting hung in the castle all these years. I stared at it for hours on end. I loved her. I regretted what happened to your mother."

Juliette's eyes flashed. "It didn't just happen. You made it happen."

Will stared at the painting. "She was a beautiful woman," said Will. "Just like you."

"Jack, is there any way you can check his story? I always wondered whether my mother was still alive and, if she was, why she never tried to find me."

"Now that we have a record of him, we will find your mother and, if his story is true, give her a proper burial. Gedeon will be locked up for a long time, for murder, art theft, and kidnapping. He won't ever hurt you again."

"Bars won't hold me." Gedeon laughed. "You think I'm afraid of your prisons?"

The ambulance pulled up to the dock.

Jack touched Kate's arm. "Go with your mother to the hospital and get her checked out. Will and I will babysit this bastard until the sun comes out, and then we'll truly see if he's a vampire. I don't believe it for a minute. I'm sure the records will show that this man is a relative, perhaps the grandson, of the man who owned the castle during the war." He turned back to Gedeon.

"One more question," Jack asked. "Was there really a threat to the European Union banking conference? Did you have anything to do with that?"

"That was just to throw you off so you'd be focused on protecting the conferees and I'd be free to conduct my business," Gedeon admitted.

"I'm going to tell the captain. They're delaying the ship. We can tell him it's okay to go on to their destination. We have our culprit. After we get Juliette checked out, we can fly back to Atlanta and you can drive back to Graysville."

"I'm not leaving without my Juliette." Will took Juliette's hand and raised it to her lips. "I plan to make our marriage official as soon as we get back home, if she'll have me."

Juliette rushed into Will's arms.

"That looks like a yes to me," Kate said, brushing off Juliette's assurances that she was okay and didn't need to go to a hospital.

"Juliette, if not for you, do it for me," Will said. Juliette finally acquiesced, and Will helped her into the ambulance. Jack asked Captain Smith to go with them to take Juliette's statement, while he waited with Will.

"I need to bring the suspect into the station," the captain objected. He had dispatched another police unit, which had just arrived on the scene.

"Give us until morning, and then he's all yours," Jack said.

"My man will wait here on the boat with you, then."

"That's fine," Jack agreed.

Jack started making calls to Interpol and the Hungarian police.

Hours passed. The "vampire" had fainted. He couldn't stand the pain.

Jack's cell phone rang. Jack, yawning and rubbing his eyes, answered it.

"I see. Yes, I understand." He spoke with the party on the other end for about fifteen minutes. Will looked up, his head bobbing from lack of sleep.

The sun was about to rise over the ocean. The rosy pinks and blue hues of the dawn were magnificent, but the men didn't pay much attention.

Jack said to Will, "I just got off the phone with the Hungarian police. They did find the body of a woman, about the age Juliette's mother was when Juliette says she left Hungary. She was hanging, or what's left of her was hanging, in chains in a dungeon below the castle.

They will do DNA testing to identify the body, or rather, the bones. Then, if it is truly Juliette's mother, we can have her sent to Atlanta for burial. Even more bizarre, she was dressed in a wedding gown. It was tattered, moth-eaten, practically in shreds. As decayed as the woman wearing it. And the bastard just left her there to rot. There were records, a diary," Jack added. "He's sending it to me in Atlanta, but there were frequent mentions of a woman named Marika. She had a daughter, Ilona. Ilona must be Juliette."

Will nodded. "She did mention that name to me on the ship."

"But something else that was strange. The name of the castle's owner was Gedeon, but according to the diary he was also the owner during World War II and the first World War and even back in earlier centuries. There was never a record of a son, no heirs, no mention of any family, or anyone but Gedeon. He seems to be a shadowy figure, and I don't believe in vampires, but this man is apparently the same man that's lived there in that castle for many centuries."

"Well the sun is about to rise. I guess we'll find out."

Will picked up a bucket of water and threw it in splashes onto Gedeon until he regained consciousness. He looked up fearfully at the sun beginning to peek through the clouds.

"Release me. I answered your questions. If you don't let me go, I'll burn to death."

Will looked at Jack, and they both looked at Gedeon, still lashed to the steering wheel by Will's silver handcuffs.

The sun beat down on the yacht, and Gedeon's skin

began to crackle and smoke.

Jack's eyes widened. "Do you believe what we're seeing? We can't just let him burn to death."

Gedeon held their gaze and fixed them with a murderous look. He began a relentless chant in an unfamiliar language, pleading and calling on someone above.

Suddenly the sky directly above the vessel was ablaze with a column of heavenly light, not sunlight but brighter, more ethereal.

Jack was stunned, locked in a trance. Will was knocked back on his feet.

When they came to, the only thing left of Gedeon were the silver cuffs, still attached to the steering wheel.

"I think I was struck by lightning," Jack said, rubbing his jaw. "I couldn't move. Must have been some kind of freak sunstorm."

"Whatever it was, it flattened me, too," Will said. "I didn't see what happened. Where did he go?"

They tried to question the police officer, who had collapsed on the deck, but though he was still breathing, he was incoherent.

Jack shrugged. "He just disappeared. I don't know whether that flash was godly or ungodly, whether he was a fallen angel or a devil or whether he was truly a vampire."

Will couldn't shed any light on the subject. "Juliette says he was delusional, that he thought she was Marika, her mother. She wasn't convinced he was a real vampire, but Gedeon was convinced of it, she's sure. What will we tell Juliette and Kate?"

"That it's over, that we're finally going home."

"But is it, Jack? Is he really gone? Will he come back for Juliette, or take revenge on us?"

"We've recovered the stolen paintings, and we know where the two in Bermuda are. The police have taken over the castle in Hungary, and the place is a crime scene, so even if he is still alive or undead or whatever it is that vampires are, he can't go back there. They'll have a warrant out for his arrest. They found more than one body in that dungeon. Apparently Gedeon or whoever he is has been plaguing that town since the seventeenth century. He was a major landowner. I can't wait to get my hands on a copy of that diary. I imagine it will make fascinating reading. The police are going to fax over some of the more relevant pages. The diaries start in 1625, and he'll fax me some of the early entries as well as those during the World War II period, to help us settle our art theft case.

"Apparently, the count had a comprehensive listing of all the paintings stored in the castle, including the ones he bought and sold over the years. He kept detailed records of who he sold them to and the compensation he received. That will help the authorities track down and return some of the stolen art. I also asked for copies of the pages around the time when he imprisoned Marika. Maybe I can get some of the answers Juliette needs. But I don't think it's a good idea for her to see the actual diary. If the woman they found in the dungeon was her mother, it would be hard for her to read it."

"She's a strong woman," Will pointed out. "I think you underestimate her. I just want to make sure Juliette will be safe."

"As far as we know, the man, or vampire, or

whoever he was, is gone," Jack said. "Did he burn up? Is he finally dead? Who can tell? It's a mystery we may never solve."

Chapter Twenty-Nine

Jack sat on a couch in the waiting room at the hospital in Bermuda, while Will paced.

"Is Kate still in with Juliette? What's taking so them so long? Why hasn't the doctor released her?"

Jack flashed a reassuring smile. "I'm sure everything is fine, or we would have heard by now. Why don't you sit down? There's something I'd like to discuss with you."

Will turned and sat on the couch next to Jack.

"It's obvious you care a lot for Juliette."

"I love her, Jack. I know it hasn't been that long, but these things happen. I've been alone for years, and her life hasn't been easy. I think we could be good for each other. She makes my heart happy."

"I'm glad, and I think you would be good for each other. That's one of the reasons I wanted to talk with you. Have you ever thought about what you're going to do once we get back to Atlanta? Your job and your life is in Graysville, and I doubt Juliette will ever leave Kate, especially now. You don't know yet, but Kate and I are having a baby. That is, Kate is having a baby, but the thing is, Juliette is going to be a grandmother."

Will shook Jack's hand. "Congratulations. That's great news."

"Thanks. We couldn't be happier. If you have any idea of getting serious with Juliette, I thought you should know what you're up against."

"I'm willing to do anything, anything, to see if there's a chance for us."

"Then I think you're going to like my proposition."

"What kind of proposition?" Will asked, keeping an eye on the hall where Juliette's room was located.

"The Crystal & Hale agency is growing. As we solve more cases, our agency is becoming more prominent, and we're getting busier. Right now, there's only Kate and me, and Juliette, and their psychic talents are a great help, but neither of them have law enforcement expertise. The thing is, I need another investigator. A man I can trust, a man I can count on to help carry the load. I would like that man to be you, Will."

"You're offering me a job?"

"I sure could use your help. I know you'd be giving up a lot, leaving Graysville. You're the big fish in a little pond, and we're only a small agency now, but we're beginning to get a national—even an international—reputation, and I think we work well together. We can learn a lot from each other. The work is exciting, nothing run of the mill. I'll make it worth your while."

Will didn't hesitate or take any time to think it over. "Since my wife died and my mama passed, I don't have any real ties or obligations in Graysville. I love that town, but my term is almost up, and I was just deciding whether or not to run again. I'm not in it for the money, but they just lowered the salaries of all the elected officials in the county. There are plenty of good men who could run and do a great job. He's young yet, but Luke Slaughter is a fine officer, for instance, and he's studying to be a lawyer. He's got brains enough for both of us. Got to make room for the next generation. I could convince him to run. It may be time for me to hang up my hat, so to speak. But I've still got a lot of good years left in me. I've enjoyed working on this case more than any case I've had since I've been on the force. And it would give Juliette and me more time together. To get to know each other. For her to decide whether she really wants a future with me. I could make her happy, Jack. I know I could."

Will got up from the couch when he saw Kate and Juliette coming toward them. "I should probably talk it over with Juliette before I commit, make sure she's on board. Make sure she doesn't mind having me around on a permanent basis. Because I plan to marry that woman."

Chapter Thirty

The Nagy Chronicles

1625—I met the count when he was still a baron and before his sons became princes, while he was head of a minor noble family in the northern part of the kingdom of Hungary. He was dashing and brash, and I was a young, impressionable soldier in his charge. It didn't matter that I was about to marry Marika, a girl I had been in love with since childhood. A girl who swore her love to me.

The count had his eye on me and, one night, after a particularly bloody battle and an even sweeter victory, when we were both exhausted and were under the influence of too much to drink, he professed his feelings. I thought of Marika, but the count and I were brothers in arms. We had sworn to die for each other. That night, what followed seemed a most natural course of action. In return for my body and my lifelong loyalty, he offered me his love, his protection, his family name, his wealth, a title, and the gift of immortality. When he put his mark on me, he was my first, for Marika and I had not yet lain together.

And although I never would have imagined wanting what we had together, it was a glorious night. A night I will always remember. And indeed, I did love him, first in the way a soldier loves his commander, but then in a more intimate and intense way. A carnal love, born of lust. But that love changed me. After that, I was no longer the man Marika fell in love with, and I had to turn away from her, for her own protection. She was shocked and shattered. Eventually, she married someone else, and I moved in with the count, in his castle on the hill. I never stopped loving Marika and sometimes, in the middle of the night, I would come down from the castle to visit her. She never knew I was there, or that I had to live with the pain of watching her with another man—her husband and her beautiful daughters—and I continued to watch her, and watch over her, until the day she died.

And what of my count, my sire, the man who initiated me into his secret brood? He went on to marry and start a dynasty, to live in other, richer castles, and he left me in mine. Eventually, we grew apart, but for his occasional visits, which always left me wanting more. Wanting more comfort. Missing his company and companionship, and also missing my first true love. And wondering whether things would have been different if I had stayed with Marika and lived a normal human life. Those centuries were some of the longest and the loneliest, and I'm afraid I developed some vile habits that made me ashamed. I cavorted with my kind in a number of empty, mind-numbing relationships, and engaged in other liaisons to try to recapture the human love I had with Marika, some by mutual consent and others, yes, often, by force when it suited me and my victim was unwilling. But I am what I am. And there is no going back. In my world, there are no second chances. There was no one I cared to share eternity with. I was known by many names through many lifetimes. But the given name Gedeon caught my fancy. The Devastater. So that identity stuck. For my family name, I kept the name of my noble sire, Nagy, which in Hungarian means a large and powerful person.

1945—By the end of World War II, while many of the royal landowners were displaced, jailed or deported, I joined the Arrow Cross, a Hungarian Fascist movement aligned with the German Nazis, that seized power in 1944. At first, it was just a diversion, but it turned out to be a wise decision, since my castle and all surrounding lands were spared. And then I began to enjoy the night forays into Budapest. We would roam the streets in our green uniforms and badges—a set of crossed arrows—and rob, terrorize, and slaughter the unfortunate locals.

My home was a fortress, so the castle was the ideal storage depot for the Nazis' stolen loot, as were the salt mines, cellars, convents, and other safehouses that had been earmarked by the Reich. And when the Soviet troops drove the Nazis out of Hungary, they left behind vast stores of treasures—thousands of sculptures, paintings, watercolors, furniture, and other priceless art and antiquities looted and seized from Italy and France and museums throughout Europe. No one knew about my secret cache, and because I had enough money to pay off the Soviets, my castle and all my holdings were spared. I was a survivor, in the strictest sense of the word.

I was a patron of the arts, and I had recovered these precious works of art. Every day, I would enter the storage rooms in the castle and catalog the treasures— landscapes, skylines, and portraits by Van Gogh, Matisse, Degas, Picasso, Chagall, Vermeer. The list was endless, as were the opportunities to unload the masterpieces to "collectors" to finance the upkeep of the castle.

1983—I had all the riches in the world but no one to share them with. There were many women, of course, and men, over the years. I had needs, after all. But none captured my heart or heated my blood like my Marika, my first love. So when I first laid eyes on a beautiful gypsy camped outside my castle, I knew she was Marika incarnated and that, by some great miracle, she had returned to me. She was the image of Marika, right down to her beckoning violet eyes and coal black hair. I had to make this woman mine. She didn't remember me, or what we had together, so she was shy at first. How could I tell her we had met in another lifetime? Where could I find the words? How could I tell her we were destined to be together? I didn't want to scare her away. So, even though I was impatient to bed her, I courted her until she seemed to develop genuine feelings for me.

I vowed to be her protector, and, with a young daughter to feed and no means of support, at first she was receptive when I wooed her. She said another man had made similar promises and did nothing to protect her when his wife sent her away. I was jealous of that man, but I held my temper. Instead, I gave her gifts and treasures and spoke to her of my love. I even had her portrait painted—a portrait of Marika and her daughter—so I could look upon her beauty anytime I pleased.

And I was happy with her, until one day she noticed my eyes wandering to Ilona. Marika's daughter was growing more lovely and ripe each day. And I wanted to taste her, just a sample, for she reminded me of a younger Marika, and I desired her. Marika pulled away from me because she didn't understand my hunger and my needs. But she knew I was powerful, and that I would get my way eventually, and that nothing she could say would stop me. She agreed to marry me if I would leave her daughter alone. I was delirious. Finally, I would be reunited with my true love.

But all those centuries of corruption made it impossible for me to resist the temptation, impossible for me to be denied. I sent my guards to pick up the child and bring her to me for a closer inspection. I told them to tell her mother I only wanted to make the child feel welcome in our home, that I had a special dress I wanted her to wear to the wedding, and a special room picked out just for her in the castle, close to ours. There were preparations to be made, and I wanted her to be a part of them. I paced my bedroom, stroking my beard and rubbing my thumb across my bottom lip in anticipation of my juicy pre-wedding appetizer.

They marched down the hill, and when they returned empty-handed, reporting the child had vanished, I'm afraid I lost my temper, and Marika paid the price. I thought Marika would come around, eventually, and tell me where the child was, but no amount of torture or pain or starvation made a dent in her defiance and, one day, when I had her brought to my bedroom, it was her body I held, but her spirit had already left this earth, before I could make her mine forever. I thought we were going to share everything. But my true love was gone from me again. And I vowed that if I ever found Ilona, I would put my brand on her so I wouldn't have to face eternity alone.

I spent countless restless nights and countless florints searching for Ilona. I hunted her down in the dark throughout Europe and all over the world, but I never found her. It was almost as if she had disappeared from the face of the earth, without a trace. No doubt her mother had woven a protective spell over her daughter, shielding her from my sight. For Marika had powerful magic, which she undoubtedly passed on to her daughter. I'd lost Marika, and without Ilona to replace her, I knew I would never be content. I would never be at peace. So I continued to search…

****

Jack put down the transcripts of the diary and rubbed his eyes.

"If Gedeon is still alive and breathing in this world, in whatever form, he'll never give up trying to find her," Will lamented. "I'll have to keep a close watch on Juliette."

"And Kate," added Jack, thinking also of the precious new life she was carrying. "I hope to God we're rid of the beast forever."

Chapter Thirty-One

Lost and Found

Somewhere, in a lamplit room, powered by the pulse of an amethyst amulet, a lone woman types a list of artists' names on a dusty, clunky, but reliable portable typewriter. The list, smudged in places, of great masters and modern artists from this school and that, an untraceable list, too sensitive to appear in any computer database, will be couriered to a certain address. And the paintings will make their way back to this museum and that, to the households of this descendant or that dealer.

Just a list. Not the golden tones of a Rembrandt or a glint of gold from a Klimt or the flash of light from a Monet. Just a name, a hint of the value finally restored to the art world. A repair, to the rent in civilization, that will occur when the missing masterpieces are delivered to their final destination.

Lost and stolen paintings suddenly, miraculously, find their way back to their proper places in the world. Appearing as mysteriously as they disappeared. The woman knows nothing more than the name of the man who will come by for the list. She has her assignment, as have many others in a long chain.

Epilogue

One Year Later

Juliette bounced baby Aurora Dawn Hale on her lap. She loved playing with her brand-new granddaughter, and so did her new husband, who had taken to calling himself Granddaddy Will. They were babysitting their little angel while Kate and Jack were out on a date, hopefully busy making more grandchildren.

"Now, Juliette, don't you go filling Aurora Dawn's head with any ideas, like how to turn her granddaddy into a frog, or worse."

Juliette smiled. "I would never dream of teaching her to do anything like that, as long as you behave yourself. But she does have psychic talent. You can tell already. She's going to surpass her mother and her grandmother. The other day, a crow flew down from the sky and landed on the side of her stroller. She reached out to pet it, and they came to an understanding. But I'm going to take it slow. She's only a baby. She'll have plenty of time to discover her abilities. She needs a chance to have a normal childhood, play games, hear stories."

Will got down on Aurora Dawn's level and looked into her violet eyes, eyes the same color as Kate's and Juliette's, and ruffled her black ringlets with his fingers.

The baby already had a full head of hair, and she was a stunner. She certainly had her granddaddy under her spell.

"Now, Aurora Dawn, Granddaddy Will is going to tell you a special story," he began. "It's a fairy tale, really." Aurora Dawn looked up into his face, and she really seemed to be listening.

"There once was a beautiful gypsy princess who fell under the spell of an evil sorcerer. The mother of the princess foretold that although her life would be difficult, one day she would be happy and meet her true love. That would be me, your Granddaddy Will."

Aurora Dawn smiled and wrapped her tiny hand around Will's finger while Romeo, Kate's Bichon Frise, sat calmly at Will's side, his paws on Will's shoes, guarding the baby.

"The beautiful princess fell head over heels in love with the handsome chief of police when they met in the faraway land of Graysville. They got married and lived happily ever after."

Juliette smiled and dangled her amethyst necklace in front of Aurora Dawn's face, and the baby pulled at the chain. At her touch, the stone glowed, and Aurora Dawn giggled.

"That is a sign of your ultimate power, little one. This amulet will be yours one day, Aurora Dawn, and you will be the most fabulous, most mystical, most beautiful, and most powerful princess in all the land. And you will have the happiest life. And one day, you will meet your prince and find true love, just like I did."

A word about the author...

Marilyn Baron is a corporate public relations consultant in Atlanta. She's a PRO member of Romance Writers of America (RWA) and Georgia Romance Writers (GRW) and winner of the GRW 2009 Chapter Service Award and writing awards in single title, suspense romance, paranormal/fantasy, and fiction with strong romantic elements. Marilyn is a new appointee on the 2015 Roswell Reads Steering Committee.

She writes humorous coming-of-*middle*-age women's fiction, historical romantic thrillers, fantasy, and psychic suspense. She graduated from the University of Florida in Gainesville, Florida, with a Bachelor of Science in Journalism (Public Relations sequence) and a minor in Creative Writing. Born in Miami, Florida, Marilyn lives in Roswell, Georgia, with her husband and they have two daughters.

She says: What's unique about my writing? I try to inject humor into everything I write. I like to laugh, and my readers do too. I tend to feature older heroines, because, let's face it, we're not getting any younger. I love to travel. My favorite place to visit is Italy, because I studied in Florence for six months in my junior year of college.

To find out more about my books and short stories, please visit my Web site at www.marilynbaron.com.